Just KID-DING Around

Around

Telephone Pioneers Kids' Cookbook

Telephone Pioneers of America

ANSWERING THE CALL OF THOSE IN NEED

Alene White, Chapter Pioneer Administrator
Linda G. Anderson, Chapter Cookbook Chairperson

Cover design from an idea and sketch
provided by Melissa Feinstein,
daughter of Janice Feinstein, Harpeth Council

This book is a collection of our favorite recipes
which are not necessarily original recipes.

Published by Favorite Recipes Press
P.O. Box 305142, Nashville, TN 37230

First Printing: 1989, 15,000
Manufactured in the United States of America
Copyright© Telephone Pioneers of America
240 Green Hills Office Building, Nashville, TN 37215
Library of Congress Number: 89-16951
ISBN: 0-87197-254-9

INTRODUCTION

Since this is a cookbook of recipes submitted by young people for dishes to be prepared by young people, it is only fitting that it should be dedicated to those Pioneers who have been, and are so, active in service to children.

We, therefore, dedicate this book to those many members, Life Members, Future Pioneers and Partners, who have devoted numerous hours to making toys, raising funds, and conducting parties for Children's Hospitals, Day Care Centers, "Just Say No" Clubs and Adopt-A-Schools, ...those people who are constantly "answering the call of those in need" and whose particular motto is

"No man stands so tall
As when he kneels
To listen to a child."

Ermon W. C. Lature
Chapter President

ACKNOWLEDGEMENTS

The Telephone Pioneers of America are grateful for the support of the many individuals who helped in the production of this cookbook. "Just Kid-ding Around" is a compilation of favorite recipes of children representing members of Tennessee Telephone Pioneers of America Chapter 21 families. The Tennessee Telephone Pioneers would especially like to recognize the following contributors:

Natalie Adcock — daughter of Diana Adcock, Green Hills Council
Jason Adkins — son of Mary Adkins, Green Hills Council
Joel Alderson — son of Cheryl Alderson, Columbia Council
Monica Lynn Barnes — stepdaughter of Thresa C. Barnes, Green Hills Council
Gary Bernard, Jr. — son of Gary and Mary Bernard, Green Hills Council
Russell Bernard — son of Gary and Mary Bernard, Green Hills Council
Amber Cher Brooks — daughter of Janis C. Brooks, Harpeth Council
Angela Brown — daughter of Paula Brown, Green Hills Council
Joshua Bryant — grandchild of Dorothy M. Bryant, Clarksville Council
Sarah Bryant — grandchild of Dorothy M. Bryant, Clarksville Council
Tiffany Connolly — daughter of Lisa Connolly, Andrew Jackson Council
Crystal Connolly — daughter of Lisa Connolly, Andrew Jackson Council
Jason L. Craig — son of Sarah Craig, Chattanooga Council
Kim Crawford — daughter of Tina Crawford, Harpeth Council
Sandy Cummings — daughter of Mary Cummings, Chattanooga Council
Angel Daniel — daughter of Teresa Daniel, Suburban East Council
Jennifer Dickey — grandchild of E. C. Clark, Jr., Clarksville Council
Christy Dorris — grandchild of Mildred S. Dorris, Jackson Council
Samantha Brooke Dorris — grandchild of Mildred S. Dorris, Jackson Council
Clint Dorris — son of Dottie Dorris, Jackson Council
Sarah Earle — daughter of Frank M. Earle, Nashboro Council
Wayne Earle — son of Frank M. Earle, Nashboro Council
Melissa Feinstein — daughter of Janice Feinstein, Harpeth Council
Emily Fisher — daughter of Sharon Fisher, Green Hills Council
Chad Frerer — grandchild of John and Sharon Griffith, Green Hills Council
Danielle Frerer — grandchild of John and Sharon Griffith, Green Hills Council
Laci Gambill — niece of Linda Anderson, Green Hills Council
Matthew Gant — nephew of Betty Jo Everett, Chattanooga Council
Deanna Gardenhire — grandchild of Bobbie Kelley, Green Hills Council
Trey Gardenhire — grandchild of Bobbie Kelley, Green Hills Council
Chris Green — son of Sheryl Green, Green Hills Council
Jason Greenway — son of Cherie Greenway, Knoxville West Council

Courtney Gryszko — grandchild of Jean Knowles,
Andrew Jackson Council
Zac Hill — son of Pam Chambers-Hill, Memphis Council
Alan Horn — son of Kathy Horn, Harpeth Council
Jamie Hutton — daughter of Carol Hutton, Green Hills Council
April D. Irwin — daughter of Carolyn Irwin, Chattanooga Council
Joshua Irwin — son of Carolyn Irwin, Chattanooga Council
Joe Lane — son of Stella Lane, Harpeth Council
Missy Lane — daughter of Stella Lane, Harpeth Council
LeeAnne Little — daughter of Helen Little, Memphis Council
Mandy Little — grandchild of Helen Little, Memphis Council
Beth Lowe — daughter of Debbie Lowe, Knoxville West Council
Wayne Lowe — son of Debbie Lowe, Knoxville West Council
LeAnne McCollum — grandchild of Frances Santini, Harpeth Council
Vance McCollum — grandchild of Frances Santini, Harpeth Council
Michelle D. McCuiston — daughter of Bettie H. McCuiston,
Clarksville Council
Brandon McDonald — son of Fred E. McDonald, Jr.,
Knoxville West Council
Travis McDonald — son of Fred E. McDonald, Jr.,
Knoxville West Council
Paige Melton — grandchild of Peggy M. Camp, Knoxville West Council
Patara Melton — grandchild of Peggy M. Camp, Knoxville West Council
Heidi Morrison — daughter of Carol Morrison, Harpeth Council
Lauren Naill — grandchild of Charles E. Naill, Knoxville West Council
Meridith Nealy — daughter of Linda Nealy, Harpeth Council
April Payton — grandchild of Frances Santini, Harpeth Council;
daughter of Karl Payton, Green Hills Council
Jason Payton — grandchild of Frances Santini, Harpeth Council;
son of Karl Payton, Green Hills Council
Amanda Ramsey — daughter of Mary K. Ramsey,
Andrew Jackson Council
Russell Riddle — son of Edna Riddle, Chattanooga Council
Brian Rives — son of Katherine Rives, Clarksville Council
Brandy Roder — daughter of Kathy Roder, Andrew Jackson Council
P.J. Roder, III — son of Kathy Roder, Andrew Jackson Council
Ashley Santini — grandchild of Frances Santini, Harpeth Council;
daughter of Rob Santini, Harpeth Council
Amanda Shields — daughter of Dinah Shields, Memphis Council
Tim Shields — son of Dinah Shields, Memphis Council
Holly Sullivan — daughter of Martha Sullivan, Green Hills Council
Whitney Tuttle — daughter of Nan Tuttle, Knoxville West Council
Jessica Marie Webb — grandchild of Norma K. Webb, Harpeth Council
Sasha White — grandchild of Alene and Herb White, Nashboro Council
Amanda Williams — grandchild of Mary Love Timmerman,
Green Hills Council
Jenny Willoughby — daughter of Sue Willoughby, Green Hills Council

CONTENTS

WHAT DOES IT MEAN?

Alternately . . . . . . To do one thing and then another by turns.

Batter . . . . A thick beaten mixture of ingredients to be cooked or baked.

Beat . . . . To mix fast by hand or electric mixer.

Blend . . . . To combine all ingredients gently until smooth.

Boil . . . . To heat until mixture begins to bubble.

Brown . . . . To cook until it turns brown on outside.

Chill . . . . To cool in refrigerator.

Chop . . . . To cut into small pieces.

Combine . . . . To mix ingredients together.

Constantly . . . . . . All the time.

Dilute . . . . To make thinner by adding liquid.

Dissolve . . . . To mix a dry ingredient into a liquid ingredient.

Dough . . . . A thick, sticky mixture of flour, liquids and other dry ingredients.

Drain . . . . To remove water or grease from food.

Fold . . . . To blend ingredients with lifting turning motion.

Grease . . . . To cover inside of bowl, baking dish or bottom of skillet with oil to prevent sticking.

Knead . . . . Repeated flattening movement made with heel of hands to thoroughly mix dough.

Lukewarm . . . . . . Warm to the touch.

Melt . . . . To turn a solid ingredient liquid by heating slowly.

Peel . . . . To remove skin from food.

Preheat . . . . To turn on oven to reach desired temperature before adding food.

Salt to taste . . . . . To put enough salt in food to taste good.

Sauté . . . . To cook in skillet with a small amount of butter, stirring often.

Separate eggs . . . To remove the yolk from the white of the egg.

Sift . . . . To put flour through sifter to make particles fine.

Simmer . . . . To cook over very low heat with just a little bit of movement in the liquid.

Slice . . . . To cut into even slices.

Toss . . . . To tumble ingredients lightly by lifting gently with 2 forks or spoons.

Whip . . . . To beat until thick, using a beater.

Sieve
Gelatin mold
Vegetable peeler
Pancake turner
Ice cube tray
Rolling pin
Colander
Blender
Grater
Griddle
1 cup
1/3 cup
1/2 cup
1/4 cup
Cookie cutters
Broiler pan

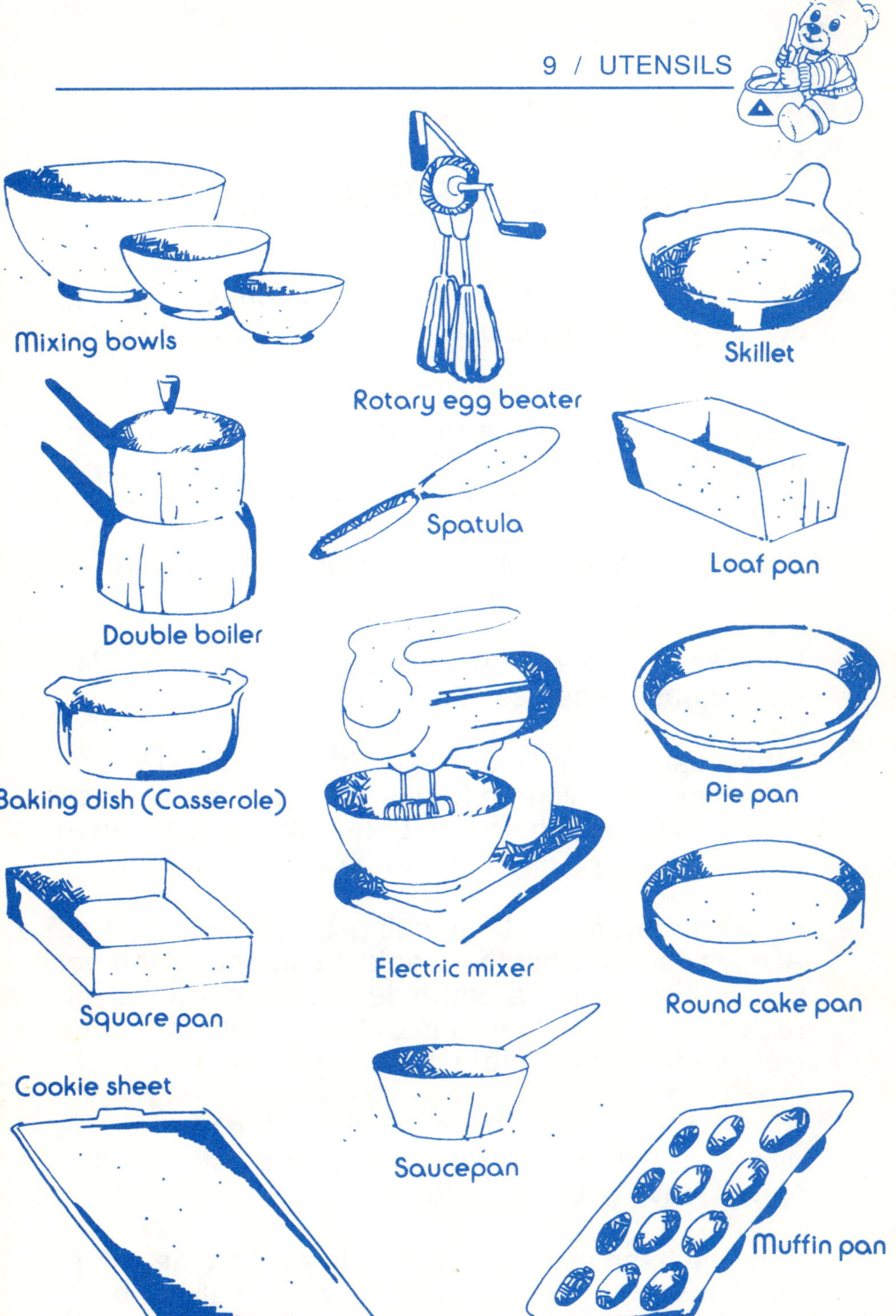

Mixing bowls
Rotary egg beater
Skillet
Double boiler
Spatula
Loaf pan
Baking dish (Casserole)
Pie pan
Electric mixer
Square pan
Round cake pan
Cookie sheet
Saucepan
Muffin pan

THINGS TO REMEMBER

- ALWAYS check with your mother before you start to cook—she's had lots of experience. Ask her to show you how to use the stove and small appliances.

- Before you start—read the recipe all the way through. Make sure you have everything you need, including ingredients and the correct utensils.

- Wash your hands and put on an apron or an old shirt—cooking can be messy.

- Use exactly the amount called for in the recipe. Use level measurements, rather than heaped up.

- When using a knife or vegetable peeler, ALWAYS cut away from yourself. Use a chopping board so you won't scratch the counter top. Never leave knives where younger children can reach them.

- Be very careful with anything that might be hot. Always use a potholder to hold the handle of the pot while stirring. Use a potholder to pull out the oven rack. Use a potholder to take things from the oven. Never set anything hot on a counter top.

- Stir a hot mixture on the stove with a wooden spoon or a metal spoon with a wooden or plastic handle. Never leave a spoon in the pan.

- Turn the handles of saucepans inward on the stove, so no one will bump the handle while walking by.

- Remember NEVER put any metal or aluminum foil in your microwave oven.

- ALWAYS plug in electrical cords with dry hands. Keep the cords out of water and away from mixer, blender and stove top.

- Use a fork for stirring dry ingredients and use a spoon for stirring liquids.

- To grease a baking dish, use a paper towel dipped in butter, margarine or cooking oil.

- Use paper towels to wipe up spills right away!

- Tap an egg against the sharp edge of the bowl just enough to crack the shell. Hold it over the bowl and with your fingers, open the crack to let the whole egg drop into the bowl.

- Hold onions under cold water while you peel them so you won't "cry".

- When you have finished cooking, make sure that the oven, burners and lights of the stove are turned off.

- Keep your kitchen as neat and clean as possible while you cook.

- LEARNING TO COOK INCLUDES LEARNING TO CLEAN UP.

HOW TO BEGIN

1.   Read the recipe all the way through.

2.   Wash your hands before you begin.

3.   Check to be sure you have all the ingredients and equipment you need.

4.   Measure the ingredients exactly as the recipe says. Use level measurements rather than heaped up.

5.   Follow the recipe step by step for the best results.

6.   Add the ingredients as they are listed in the recipe.

7.   Have a potholder at hand to hold hot utensils.

8.   Keep the kitchen as neat and clean as you can while you cook. Learning to cook also means learning to clean up.

9.   Check with your Mom or Dad when using a knife.

WHEN MEASURING, REMEMBER...

3 teaspoons = 1 tablespoon
2 tablespoons = 1/8 cup
4 tablespoons = 1/4 cup
8 tablespoons = 1/2 cup
12 tablespoons = 3/4 cup
16 tablespoons = 1 cup
5 tablespoons + 1 teaspoon = 1/3 cup
4 ounces = 1/2 cup
8 ounces = 1 cup
16 ounces = 1 pound
2 cups = 1 pint
2 pints = 1 quart
1 quart = 4 cups

Early Bird

BREAKFASTS

EGG IN A FRAME

1 slice bread
2 teaspoons butter
1 egg

Cut . . . . hole in center of bread with rim of drinking glass.

Melt . . . . 1 teaspoon butter in small skillet over low heat.

Place . . . . bread in skillet. Break egg into small bowl; slide into hole in bread. Don't worry if the yolk breaks.

Cook . . . . until bread is golden brown on the bottom and egg is partially set.

Lift . . . . egg and bread very carefully using pancake turner. Place remaining teaspoon butter in skillet. Turn egg and bread uncooked side down in skillet.

Cook . . . . for 1 to 2 minutes longer or until egg is cooked the way you like it.

Yields . . . . 1 serving.

YUMMY EGGS

4 eggs
1 cup milk
1/2 teaspoon salt
1 tablespoon melted butter

Break . . . . eggs into medium bowl. Beat with egg beater until light yellow colored and foamy.

Add . . . . milk and salt; beat until well mixed. Add butter; mix well.

Pour . . . . into top of double boiler; place over boiling water.

Cook . . . . for 20 minutes, stirring occasionally.

Yields . . . . 4 servings.

WAFFLEY CHEESE STRATA

1   8-count package frozen waffles
2 tablespoons butter, softened
1   8-ounce package sliced cheese
6 eggs, beaten
3 cups milk

Toast . . . . waffles using package directions.
Cool. Spread with butter.
Arrange . . . . several waffles in single layer in
8x12-inch baking dish. Top with
cheese slices.
Repeat . . . . layers with remaining waffles and
cheese slices.
Beat . . . . eggs with milk in medium bowl. Pour
over waffles and cheese carefully.
Cover . . . . baking dish with plastic wrap.
Chill . . . . in refrigerator for 3 hours or longer.
Preheat . . . . oven to 325 degrees.
Remove . . . . plastic wrap.
Bake . . . . strata for 35 to 40 minutes or until
golden brown.
Let . . . . stand for 5 minutes. Cut into
squares.
Yields . . . . 6 servings.

CHEESY EGG SCRAMBLE

4 eggs
1/4 cup milk
1/4 cup shredded Cheddar cheese
2 slices crisp-fried bacon, crumbled
Salt and pepper to taste
2 tablespoons butter

Break . . . . eggs into small bowl. Beat with fork until foamy.
Add . . . . milk, cheese, bacon and salt and pepper; mix well.
Melt . . . . butter in skillet over medium heat.
Add . . . . egg mixture gradually.
Cook . . . . until eggs are set, stirring frequently with fork.
Yields . . . . 3 to 4 servings.

FLAVORED BUTTERS

Cinnamon Butter

1 pound butter, softened
1 pound confectioners' sugar
3 tablespoons cinnamon

Combine . . . . . softened butter, confectioners' sugar and cinnamon in mixer bowl.
Beat . . . . with electric mixer at medium speed until smooth and creamy.
Serve . . . . on toast, pancakes, or waffles.
Store . . . . remaining Cinnamon Butter in covered container in refrigerator.
Yields . . . . 2 pounds.

Strawberry Butter

1   10-ounce package frozen strawberries, thawed
1 cup confectioners' sugar
1 cup butter, softened

Combine . . . . . strawberries, confectioners' sugar and butter in blender container.
Place . . . . cover on container.
Process . . . . . . on High until smooth.
Serve . . . . on toast, pancakes, or waffles.
Store . . . . remaining Strawberry Butter in covered container in refrigerator.
Yields . . . . 1 1/4 pounds.

YUMMY CINNAMON TOAST

4 slices bread
2 tablespoons butter
1 to 2 teaspoons cinnamon
1/2 cup sugar

Preheat . . . . oven to 400 degrees.
Place . . . . bread slices on baking sheet.
Dot . . . . slices with butter cut into small
                        pieces.
Sprinkle . . . . . . with cinnamon to taste.
Cover . . . . each slice with 2 tablespoons sugar.
Bake . . . . until crust is brown and sugar and
                        butter are bubbly.
Yields . . . . 4 slices.

✏ **More Yummy Fun**

Orange Cinnamon Toast — Mix 2 tablespoons
     frozen orange juice concentrate, 1/2 cup sugar,
     2 teaspoons cinnamon and 2 tablespoons
     melted butter in small bowl. Spread on 8 slices
     white bread. Place on baking sheet. Bake just
     like Yummy Cinnamon Toast.

PINEAPPLE UPSIDE-DOWN BREAKFAST ROLLS

1/2 cup packed brown sugar
1 stick butter, sliced
3/4 cup crushed pineapple
1 teaspoon cinnamon
1   10-count can refrigerator biscuits

Preheat . . . . oven to 425 degrees.
Place . . . . brown sugar in 8x8-inch baking pan.
Dot with butter slices.
Bake . . . . for several minutes until butter
melts. Add pineapple and cinnamon;
mix well.
Arrange . . . . biscuits over pineapple mixture.
Bake . . . . for 10 minutes or until golden brown.
Place . . . . serving plate on top of pan; turn
plate and pan upside-down carefully.
Remove pan.
Yields . . . . 10 rolls.

FRENCH TOAST

1 egg
1/3 cup milk
1 teaspoon butter
4 slices bread

Break . . . . egg into small shallow bowl. Beat with fork until foamy. Add milk; mix well.

Melt . . . . butter in skillet over low heat.

Dip . . . . 1 slice of bread at a time into egg mixture, turning to coat with mixture.

Place . . . . in skillet. Cook until golden brown on bottom; turn slice over. Cook until golden brown.

Repeat . . . . with remaining slices.

Place . . . . on serving plates.

Serve . . . . with confectioners' sugar, maple syrup or cinnamon-sugar.

Yields . . . . 4 servings.

ABC PANCAKES

1 egg, beaten
1/2 cup milk
3 tablespoons oil
1 1/4 cups sifted all-purpose flour
1 1/2 teaspoons baking powder
3/4 teaspoon salt
1 tablespoon sugar

Preheat . . . . griddle over medium heat.
Combine . . . . . egg, milk and oil in bowl; mix well.
Sift . . . . flour, baking powder, salt and sugar together onto waxed paper.
Add . . . . flour mixture to egg mixture; stir just until mixed.
Drizzle . . . . 1 teaspoonful batter at a time onto hot greased griddle to form letters.
Cook . . . . until golden brown on bottom. Turn over carefully. Cook until golden brown.
Ladle . . . . remaining batter carefully over and around letters, making pancakes of desired size.
Cook . . . . until golden brown on both sides, turning pancakes over once.
Serve . . . . with butter and pancake syrup.
Yields . . . . 12 pancakes.

JOE'S SOUR CREAM PANCAKES

1 cup all-purpose flour
1 teaspoon soda
1/2 teaspoon salt
1 to 3 tablespoons sugar
2 tablespoons melted butter
1 cup sour cream
2 eggs, beaten
1 tablespoon vanilla extract

Preheat . . . . . . griddle over medium heat.
Combine . . . . . flour, soda, salt and sugar in bowl; mix well.
Add . . . . butter, sour cream, eggs and vanilla; mix until smooth.
Ladle . . . . 2 tablespoons batter at a time onto hot greased griddle.
Cook . . . . until golden brown on bottom. Turn over carefully. Cook until golden brown.
Serve . . . . with maple syrup or fresh fruit.
Yields . . . . 16 small pancakes.

LIGHT AND CRISP BELGIAN WAFFLES

2 egg whites
2 egg yolks
2 cups milk
2 cups all-purpose flour
1/2 teaspoon salt
1 tablespoon baking powder
1/3 cup oil

Preheat . . . . Belgian waffle iron.
Beat . . . . egg whites in mixer bowl with electric mixer at high speed until stiff peaks form. Set aside.
Combine . . . . . . egg yolks, milk, flour, salt, baking powder and oil in large mixer bowl.
Beat . . . . with electric mixer at low speed until ingredients are moistened.
Beat . . . . at medium speed until smooth.
Fold . . . . in egg whites gently with spatula.
Pour . . . . 1/2 cup batter onto hot waffle grids; close waffle iron.
Bake . . . . for 2 to 2 1/2 minutes or until waffle is golden brown and tests done.
Repeat . . . . with remaining batter.
Serve . . . . with favorite waffle toppings.
Yields . . . . 18 waffles.

MONICA'S FRUIT SMOOTHIE

1 cup cold apple juice
1 banana, peeled, cut up
3 or 4 ice cubes
1 teaspoon honey

Combine . . . . . . apple juice, banana, ice cubes and honey in blender container. Place cover on container.

Process . . . . until smooth and frothy. Pour into large glass.

Yields . . . . 1 serving.

✏ **More Yummy Fun**

Special Favorite Smoothie — You can substitute any favorite fruit juice or fruit. Try this delicious drink with strawberries, peaches or pineapple.

A BERRY GOOD BANANA SMOOTHIE

2 bananas
2 cups fresh strawberries
1 cup milk
1 cup plain yogurt

Peel . . . . and chop bananas. Rinse the strawberries and pat dry; remove stems.

Combine . . . . . . bananas, strawberries, milk and yogurt in blender container. Place cover on container.

Process . . . . until smooth. Pour into glasses.

Yields . . . . 2 or 3 servings.

✐ More Yummy Fun

Apple Advantage Smoothie — Omit milk and yogurt and add 1/2 cup apple juice, 1 cup crushed ice and 1 tablespoon honey. Process as above.

"M&M's" Powered Smoothie — Reduce milk to 1/2 cup, substitute 1/2 cup vanilla ice cream for yogurt and add small package of "M&M's" Chocolate Candies and about 1/2 cup crushed ice. Process as above.

Time Out For

LUNCH

HOT DOG DOTTED TOMATO SOUP

1   10-ounce can tomato soup
1 soup can milk
3 hot dogs
3 tablespoons Parmesan cheese

Place . . . . soup in medium saucepan.
Add . . . . milk a little at a time, stirring until soup is smooth.
Cook . . . . over medium heat until hot, stirring frequently. Do not let soup boil.
Slice . . . . hot dogs into thin circles. Add to hot soup.
Cook . . . . over medium heat for 5 minutes longer. Do not let soup boil.
Ladle . . . . into soup bowls.
Sprinkle . . . . . . Parmesan cheese over top of soup.
Yields . . . . 3 servings.

✏ **More Yummy Fun**

Make-Your-Favorite-Soup — Use cream of celery or cream of mushroom or split pea soup instead of tomato. Or use chopped ham or lunch meat instead of hot dogs.

MICROWAVE CREAMY PEANUT SOUP

1 small onion, chopped
1 stalk celery, chopped
2 tablespoons butter
4½ teaspoons flour
4 cups canned chicken broth
1 cup peanut butter
1 cup half and half
¼ cup chopped peanuts

Combine . . . . . . onion, celery and butter in 2-quart glass casserole.
Microwave . . . on High for 3 minutes.
Add . . . . flour; mix well. Pour chicken broth into casserole very slowly, stirring constantly.
Cover . . . . casserole with plastic wrap.
Microwave . . . on High for 6 minutes. Stir every 2 minutes.
Add . . . . peanut butter and half and half; mix until well blended.
Microwave . . . on Medium for 6 to 8 minutes. Do not let soup boil.
Ladle . . . . into soup bowls.
Sprinkle . . . . . . peanuts on top.
Yields . . . . 6 servings.

HOT PEANUT BUTTER AND JELLY SANDWICH

2 slices bread
1 to 2 tablespoons peanut butter
2 teaspoons favorite jelly
1 teaspoon butter

Spread . . . . 1 slice bread with peanut butter and jelly. Top with remaining bread slice.
Melt . . . . half the butter in skillet over medium heat. Place sandwich in skillet.
Cook . . . . until golden brown on bottom.
Lift . . . . sandwich carefully with pancake turner.
Melt . . . . remaining butter in skillet.
Turn . . . . sandwich over to place uncooked side down in skillet.
Cook . . . . until golden brown.
Serve . . . . warm with big glass of cold milk.
Yields . . . . 1 serving.

✏ **More Yummy Fun**

Peanut Butter And Raisin Sandwich — Spread 2 slices whole wheat bread with peanut butter. Sprinkle 1/4 cup raisins over peanut butter on 1 slice and top with remaining slice. Eat cold or hot as above.

WHOPPER CHEESEBURGERS

2 pounds ground beef
2 tablespoons instant minced onion
Salt and pepper to taste
6 slices cheese
6 hamburger buns

Combine . . . . . . ground beef, minced onion and salt and pepper in bowl; mix well.
Shape . . . . into 6 patties. Place on rack in broiler pan.
Broil . . . . for 10 minutes. Turn patties over.
Place . . . . cheese slice on each pattie.
Broil . . . . for 1 minute or until cheese melts.
Place . . . . on hamburger buns.
Add . . . . your favorite cheeseburger toppings.
Yields . . . . 6 servings.

✏ **More Yummy Fun**

Surprise Cheeseburgers — Prepare ground beef as above. Shape into 12 thin patties. Place cheese slice on each of 6 patties, top with remaining patties and seal edges of patties together to hide cheese. Broil patties for 5 to 6 minutes on each side.

HOT DIGGETY DOGS

1   8-count package refrigerator crescent rolls
8 hot dogs
4 slices American cheese

Preheat . . . . oven to 400 degrees.
Unroll . . . . and separate crescent roll dough.
Place . . . . 1 hot dog and ½ slice cheese on
                     wide end of each roll.
Roll . . . . up hot dog and cheese in roll dough.
Place . . . . point down on lightly greased baking
                     sheet.
Bake . . . . for 10 minutes or until golden brown.
Serve . . . . hot with mustard, mayonnaise and
                     pickles.
Yields . . . . 8 servings.

PAC MAN SANDWICH

1 slice bologna
2 slices bread

Make . . . . cut in bologna slice from center to outer edge. Place on plate.

Microwave . . . on High until bologna is cooked to your taste. Bologna will shrink while cooking to leave a space between the cut edges so that bologna slice resembles Pac Man.

Place . . . . bologna on 1 slice bread. Add any of your favorite extras such as catsup, mustard, mayonnaise, lettuce, tomato and pickle. Top with the remaining bread slice.

Yields . . . . 1 serving.

PARTY SANDWICHES

6 slices bread
2 to 3 tablespoons tuna salad
2 to 3 tablespoons chicken salad
2 to 3 tablespoons pimento cheese

Make . . . . 1 tuna salad sandwich, 1 chicken
salad sandwich and 1 pimento
cheese sandwich.

Cut . . . . 1 sandwich diagonally from corner to
corner to make 4 triangles. Cut 1
sandwich into 4 finger-sized bars.
Cut 1 sandwich into 4 squares.

Arrange . . . . sandwiches attractively on serving
plate.

Yields . . . . 3 to 4 servings.

✏ **More Yummy Fun**

Zoowiches — Cut sandwiches into animal shapes
with cookie cutters. You may eat the trimmings
before serving.

Conewiches — Serve tuna salad, chicken salad or
pimento cheese in miniature ice cream cones.

TUNA SALAD SANDWICHES

1   6-ounce can tuna
3 hard-boiled eggs, grated
1/4 cup sweet salad cubes
1/4 cup (or more) mayonnaise
12 to 14 slices bread

Drain . . . . tuna; place in bowl. Flake with fork.
Add . . . . eggs, salad cubes and enough
mayonnaise to make mixture
spreadable; mix well.
Spread . . . . tuna salad on half the bread slices;
top with remaining bread slices.
Trim . . . . crusts from sandwiches; cut each
sandwich into 4 squares.
Serve . . . . sandwiches with favorite potato or
corn chips.
Yields . . . . 6 to 7 servings.

TUNA HERO

2   6-ounce cans tuna
1/4 cup chopped celery
2 tablespoons sweet pickle relish
1/2 cup mayonnaise
1 loaf French bread
3 slices sharp Cheddar cheese

Drain . . . . tuna; place in bowl. Flake with fork.

Add . . . . celery, relish and mayonnaise; mix
well with fork.

Split . . . . French bread horizontally. Cut
cheese slices into triangles.

Spread . . . . tuna salad on cut side of bottom half
of loaf.

Add . . . . lettuce, cheese triangles and top of
loaf. May secure top with toothpick if
necessary.

Cut . . . . loaf diagonally into 6 sandwiches.

Yields . . . . 6 servings.

EASY MINI PIZZAS

1   10-count can refrigerator biscuits
1   8-ounce can tomato sauce
3 ounces sliced pepperoni
1 to 2 cups shredded mozzarella cheese

Preheat . . . . oven to 400 degrees.
Flatten . . . . biscuits 1 at a time between palms of hands; place on baking sheet.
Spread . . . . tomato sauce over biscuits.
Arrange . . . . pepperoni slices on top; sprinkle with cheese.
Bake . . . . for 8 to 10 minutes or until cheese is melted and bubbly.
Yields . . . . 10 servings.

JACK-O'LANTERN PIZZAS

4 English muffins, split
1   8-ounce can pizza sauce
8 slices cheese

Preheat . . . . . . oven to 400 degrees.
Separate . . . . . muffins. Toast until brown.
Spread . . . . about 1 tablespoon pizza sauce on each muffin.
Trim . . . . off corners of cheese slices to make circles to fit muffins.
Cut . . . . jack-o'lantern face in each circle; remove cutouts and place cheese circle on muffins. You may eat the cutouts if you wish.
Place . . . . on baking sheet.
Bake . . . . for several minutes until cheese is melted.
Yields . . . . 8 servings.

This recipe can also be baked in a toaster oven.

PEANUT BUTTER HONEY BUNS

4 hot dog buns, split
1/4 cup creamy peanut butter
1 or 2 bananas, sliced
4 teaspoons honey
4 teaspoons sunflower seed

Spread . . . . bottom half of each bun with about 1 tablespoon peanut butter.
Arrange . . . . . . banana slices over peanut butter. Drizzle honey over bananas.
Sprinkle . . . . sunflower seed over honey and add bun top.
Yields . . . . 4 servings.

BUNNY FOOD

2 pounds carrots
1 bunch celery
1 large green bell pepper
1 large cucumber
2 pints cherry tomatoes

Wash . . . . all vegetables well; drain on paper towels.
Cut . . . . carrots, celery and green pepper into strips; place in large bowl.
Cut . . . . cucumber into 1/4-inch slices; place in bowl.
Add . . . . tomatoes; toss vegetables lightly.
Chill . . . . until serving time.
Serve . . . . vegetables plain for munching or with a favorite dip.
Yields . . . . 20 servings.

EASY FRUIT SALAD

1   16-ounce can fruit cocktail
2 bananas, sliced
1 cup flaked coconut

Drain . . . . fruit cocktail; place fruit in bowl.
Add . . . . bananas and coconut; mix gently.
Chill . . . . until serving time.
Yields . . . . 6 servings.

✏ **More Yummy Fun**

Fresh Fruit Salad — Substitute 2 or 3 cups of your favorite fresh fruit cut into bite-sized pieces for fruit cocktail.

RAGGEDY ANN SALAD

1 canned peach half
1/2 hard-boiled egg
4 small celery sticks
1 leaf curly lettuce
1/4 cup finely shredded cheese
1/4 maraschino cherry
Raisins

Place . . . . peach in center of salad plate.
Position . . . . . . egg for head, celery sticks for arms
and legs and lettuce for skirt.
Add . . . . cheese for hair, cherry for mouth
and raisins for eyes, nose, buttons
and shoes.
Yields . . . . 1 serving.

PEANUT BUTTER AND BANANA SHAKE

1 banana
1/4 cup creamy peanut butter
1 cup vanilla ice cream
1 cup milk

Combine . . . . . banana, peanut butter, ice cream and milk in blender container. Place cover on container.
Process . . . . . . until smooth and creamy.
Pour . . . . into frosty glasses.
Yields . . . . 2 servings.

✏ **More Yummy Fun**

Snappy Apple Shake — Substitute 3/4 cup smooth or chunky applesauce for banana.

Choconana Shake — Substitute chocolate ice cream for vanilla.

FRUITY CRUSH

1   6-ounce can frozen orange juice concentrate, thawed
1   6-ounce can frozen grape juice concentrate, thawed
1   6-ounce can lemonade concentrate, thawed
4 cups water
1 quart ginger ale, chilled

Combine . . . . . . juice concentrates and water in large pitcher; mix well.
Chill . . . . until serving time.
Add . . . . ginger ale gradually; stir gently.
Fill . . . . tall glasses about $2/3$ full with crushed ice.
Pour . . . . juice mixture over ice.
Yields . . . . 10 servings.

CHOOSE-A-FLAVOR SHERBET

1 cup sugar
1 envelope unsweetened drink mix powder
3 cups milk

Mix . . . . sugar and drink mix powder in
medium bowl.
Add . . . . milk gradually, stirring until sugar
and drink mix are dissolved.
Pour . . . . into freezer tray. Freeze until slushy.
Spoon . . . . into mixer bowl. Beat with electric
mixer at medium speed until smooth.
Return to freezer tray.
Freeze . . . . for 2 hours or until firm.
Yields . . . . 5 or 6 servings.

☞ **More Yummy Fun**

Chunky Fruit Sherbet — Stir 1 to 2 cups chopped
fresh fruit into sherbet after beating until smooth.

ICE CREAM SANDWICHES

1 roll refrigerator chocolate cookie dough
1 roll refrigerator chocolate chip cookie dough
1 quart (or more) chocolate mint ice cream,
  softened

Preheat . . . . oven to 350 degrees.
Slice . . . . cookie dough; place on cookie sheet.
Bake . . . . according to package directions.
  Cool.
Spread . . . . ice cream 1/2 to 3/4 inch thick on
  chocolate cookies.
Top . . . . with chocolate chip cookies.
Wrap . . . . each cookie in foil; seal tightly.
Store . . . . in freezer.
Yields . . . . 3 dozen.

Little Helper

DINNERS

BAKED SPAGHETTI

1 pound ground beef
1/2 cup chopped onion
1 clove of garlic, chopped
1   16-ounce jar spaghetti sauce
Salt and pepper to taste
1   8-ounce package spaghetti
2 cups shredded Cheddar cheese

Preheat . . . . oven to 350 degrees.
Cook . . . . ground beef with onion and garlic in skillet until ground beef is brown and crumbly, stirring frequently; drain.
Mix . . . . in spaghetti sauce and add salt and pepper to taste.
Simmer . . . . for several minutes, stirring several times.
Cook . . . . spaghetti according to the package directions; drain well. Place in 9x13-inch baking dish.
Ladle . . . . spaghetti sauce over spaghetti.
Sprinkle . . . . cheese over top.
Bake . . . . for 40 minutes.
Yields . . . . 6 to 8 servings.

MEXICAN MIX CASSEROLE

1 15-ounce can chili
1 12-ounce can whole kernel corn, drained
2 cups shredded cheese
1 to 2 cups crushed nacho chips

Preheat . . . . . . oven to 350 degrees.
Pour . . . . chili into casserole. Spread corn evenly over chili.
Sprinkle . . . . . . cheese over corn.
Spread . . . . crushed nacho chips over top; press in gently.
Bake . . . . for 20 minutes or until bubbly.
Serve . . . . with additional nacho chips.
Yields . . . . 6 servings.

JASON'S TACO CASSEROLE

1 pound ground beef
1 envelope taco seasoning mix
1   16-ounce can chili beans
1   28-ounce can stewed tomatoes
1/2 cup water
1 cup shredded mozzarella cheese
1   8-ounce package corn chips
2 cups shredded Cheddar cheese

Preheat . . . . oven to 350 degrees.
Cook . . . . ground beef in skillet until brown and
crumbly, stirring frequently; drain.
Add . . . . seasoning mix, chili beans, tomatoes
and water. Mash tomatoes with
spoon; mix well.
Simmer . . . . for 5 minutes. Add mozzarella
cheese; stir until melted.
Sprinkle . . . . corn chips in 9x13-inch baking dish.
Spoon ground beef mixture over
chips. Top with Cheddar cheese.
Bake . . . . for 20 minutes or until cheese is
melted.
Yields . . . . 6 to 8 servings.

EASY MEAT LOAF

2 eggs
1/3 cup catsup
1 envelope dry onion soup mix
3 slices bread
2 pounds ground beef
3/4 cup water

Preheat . . . . . . oven to 350 degrees.
Beat . . . . eggs lightly in large bowl. Add the catsup and the soup mix; mix well.
Tear . . . . bread into small pieces; add to soup mixture; mix well.
Add . . . . ground beef and water; mix lightly until evenly mixed. Pat into loaf pan.
Bake . . . . for 1 hour. Remove to serving plate.
Let . . . . stand for 10 minutes to make slicing easier.
Yields . . . . 6 to 8 servings.

More Yummy Fun

Miniature Meat Loaves — Prepare meat loaf mixture as above. Pat into muffin cups. Bake at 350 degrees for 25 minutes. Remove from muffin cups and serve immediately.

NO-PEEK STEW

1   16-ounce can tiny peas
2 pounds cubed beef stew meat
2 potatoes, peeled, sliced
1 cup chopped carrots
1½ cups chopped onions
Salt and pepper to taste
1   10-ounce can tomato soup

Preheat . . . . . . oven to 275 degrees.
Drain . . . . peas, reserving ½ cup liquid.
Combine . . . . . drained peas, stew meat, potatoes, carrots and onions in greased 3-quart casserole; mix gently.
Sprinkle . . . . with salt and pepper.
Mix . . . . soup with reserved pea liquid in small bowl. Pour over meat and vegetables.
Cover . . . . casserole tightly with foil.
Bake . . . . for 5 hours. Do not peek.
Serve . . . . with hot biscuits or thick slices of hot crusty bread.
Yields . . . . 6 servings.

MICROWAVE ITALIAN SQUIGGLES

1 pound lean ground beef
1   15-ounce jar spaghetti sauce
2½ cups water
1   8-ounce package corkscrew pasta
Parmesan cheese

Place . . . . ground beef in colander in 2-quart glass casserole; cover with paper towel.
Microwave . . . on High for 3 minutes. Break up ground beef with wooden spoon.
Microwave . . . for 2 to 3 minutes longer or until ground beef is no longer pink.
Discard . . . . drippings. Place ground beef in glass casserole.
Add . . . . spaghetti sauce and water; mix well.
Microwave . . . on High for 6 to 7 minutes or until boiling.
Add . . . . pasta; mix well. Cover with paper towel.
Microwave . . . on High for 15 minutes or until pasta is tender, stirring every 5 minutes with wooden spoon.
Remove . . . . casserole from microwave using potholders. Let stand for 5 minutes.
Sprinkle . . . . desired amount of Parmesan cheese over top.
Yields . . . . 6 servings.

GROUND BEEF GOULASH À LA APRIL

1¹/₂ pounds ground beef
1 cup chopped onions
1   16-ounce can whole kernel corn
1   16-ounce can early June peas
2 cups catsup
¹/₂ cup steak sauce
1 teaspoon Worcestershire sauce
¹/₂ teaspoon seasoned salt
¹/₂ teaspoon barbecue spice
¹/₂ teaspoon garlic powder
Salt and pepper to taste

Cook . . . . ground beef in large skillet over medium heat until ground beef is brown and crumbly, stirring often.

Add . . . . onions. Cook until onions are brown. Drain ground beef mixture well.

Add . . . . corn, peas, catsup, steak sauce, Worcestershire sauce, seasoned salt, barbecue spice and garlic powder; mix well.

Heat . . . . until mixture comes to a boil; reduce heat to low.

Simmer . . . . uncovered, for 20 minutes, stirring occasionally.

Add . . . . salt and pepper to taste.

Yields . . . . 10 cups.

FAVORITE PIZZA

1 package dry yeast
1 cup warm water
1 teaspoon sugar
1 teaspoon salt
2 tablespoons oil
2½ cups flour

Dissolve . . . . . yeast in warm water in medium bowl. Add sugar, salt, oil and flour. Beat with wooden spoon for about 20 strokes or until well mixed.

Let . . . . dough rise, lightly covered, for 20 minutes.

Preheat . . . . oven to 375 degrees.

Divide . . . . dough into 2 portions. Roll each portion into 10-inch circle on lightly floured surface.

Place . . . . dough circles on baking sheets or fit into pizza pans.

Add . . . . your favorite pizza sauce, toppings and cheese.

Bake . . . . for 15 minutes or until crust is brown and cheese is bubbly.

Cut . . . . into wedges.

Yields . . . . 4 to 6 servings.

CHIPPY CHICKEN

2 cups potato chip crumbs
1/4 teaspoon garlic salt
Pepper to taste
1   3-pound chicken, cut up
1/2 cup melted margarine

Preheat . . . . oven to 375 degrees.
Combine . . . . . . potato chip crumbs, garlic salt and
pepper in shallow dish.
Dip . . . . chicken pieces 1 at a time into
melted margarine; roll in potato chip
crumbs until coated.
Arrange . . . . chicken pieces skin side up in 9x13-
inch baking pan.
Bake . . . . for 1 hour or until chicken is brown
and crispy.
Yields . . . . 4 servings.

GLAZED CHICKEN

1/4 cup shortening
1/4 cup catsup
1/4 cup lemon juice
2 tablespoons Worcestershire sauce
6 pieces chicken
1/4 teaspoon salt
Pinch of pepper

Preheat . . . . . . oven to 350 degrees.
Combine . . . . . shortening, catsup, lemon juice and Worcestershire sauce in saucepan. Bring to a boil, stirring occasionally; remove from heat.
Arrange . . . . chicken pieces in 9x13-inch baking pan. Sprinkle with salt and pepper. Pour sauce over chicken.
Bake . . . . for 45 minutes, turning chicken pieces several times during baking.
Yields . . . . 3 to 6 servings.

FRIED CHICKEN LEGS

Oil for frying
1 cup flour
Salt and pepper to taste
Garlic powder to taste
Thyme to taste
6 chicken legs

Pour . . . . about 1 inch oil into large skillet over low heat.

Combine . . . . . flour, salt, pepper, garlic powder and thyme in plastic bag; shake to mix well.

Add . . . . chicken legs; shake until coated with flour mixture. Remove from bag and shake off excess flour.

Place . . . . chicken legs carefully in hot oil in skillet.

Cook . . . . until golden brown and crisp, turning chicken legs carefully as necessary.

Yields . . . . 3 servings.

MICROWAVE PINEAPPLE PORK CHOPS

4 pork chops
1 teaspoon salt
1/4 teaspoon pepper
1   8-ounce can pineapple slices
3 tablespoons pineapple juice

Arrange . . . . . . pork chops in 7x11-inch glass baking dish. Sprinkle with salt and pepper.

Place . . . . pineapple slices on chops. Drizzle pineapple juice over top. Cover with plastic wrap.

Microwave . . . on Medium-High for 15 to 20 minutes or until pork chops are cooked through. Do not undercook.

Yields . . . . 2 to 4 servings.

RANCH HOUSE FISH FILLETS

1 pound frozen fish fillets
1 cup sour cream
3/4 cup mayonnaise
1 envelope dry ranch salad dressing mix
1   3-ounce can French-fried onion rings

Preheat .... oven to 350 degrees.
Arrange .... frozen fillets in shallow baking dish.
Combine ..... sour cream, mayonnaise, salad dressing mix and half the onion rings in bowl; mix well. Spoon over fillets.
Bake .... for 20 minutes. Crumble remaining onion rings over top.
Bake .... for 10 to 20 minutes longer or until fish flakes easily with fork. Ask Mom to show you how to do this test for doneness.
Yields .... 4 servings.

BAKED SALMON LOAF

1¹/₂ cups milk
1 slice bread, torn
¹/₄ cup butter
2 cups canned salmon
2 eggs
¹/₂ teaspoon salt

Preheat . . . . oven to 350 degrees.
Combine . . . . . . milk, bread and butter in top of double boiler over boiling water.
Heat . . . . until mixture is smooth and creamy, stirring frequently; remove from heat.
Place . . . . salmon in bowl. Remove salmon bones carefully. Add eggs; mix well. Add milk mixture; mix well.
Spoon . . . . into greased 5x9-inch loaf pan.
Bake . . . . for 1 hour or until firm.
Serve . . . . salmon hot or cold.
Yields . . . . 6 to 8 servings.

QUICK TUNA-MAC

1   14-ounce package macaroni and cheese mix
1   10-ounce can cream of mushroom soup
1/2 cup milk
1   6-ounce can tuna
2 cups potato chip crumbs
2 slices American cheese

Preheat . . . . oven to 350 degrees.
Cook . . . . macaroni and cheese according to the package directions. Add soup, milk and tuna; mix well.
Sprinkle . . . . half the potato chip crumbs evenly into greased 2-quart casserole. Spoon tuna mixture into casserole.
Top . . . . with remaining potato chip crumbs. Cut cheese slices into thin strips; arrange strips in decorative pattern over top.
Yields . . . . 6 servings.

HOLLY'S MACARONI AND CHEESE

1   12-ounce package macaroni
1 pound Velveeta cheese
1/2 cup butter
1 small can evaporated milk
1 cup shredded sharp Cheddar cheese

Preheat . . . . oven to 350 degrees.
Cook . . . . macaroni according to the package directions; drain well.
Cut . . . . Velveeta into cubes; place in 2-quart glass casserole. Add butter and evaporated milk.
Microwave . . . on High for 2 minutes or until cheese and butter are melted, stirring every minute.
Add . . . . macaroni; mix well. Sprinkle shredded Cheddar cheese over top.
Bake . . . . for 20 to 25 minutes or until bubbly.
Yields . . . . 6 servings.

MICROWAVE SPANISH RICE

6 slices bacon, chopped
1/4 cup finely chopped onion
1/2 cup chopped green bell pepper
3 cups cooked rice
1   16-ounce can stewed tomatoes
1 1/2 teaspoons salt
1/4 teaspoon pepper
1/2 cup shredded Cheddar cheese

Place . . . . several layers of paper towels in 2-quart glass casserole. Place bacon on towels.
Microwave . . . . on High for 3 minutes or until bacon is crisp.
Shake . . . . bacon into casserole; discard towels.
Add . . . . onion, green pepper, rice, undrained tomatoes and salt and pepper; mix well.
Microwave . . . . on High for 12 to 15 minutes or until heated through.
Sprinkle . . . . cheese over top. Let stand until cheese melts.
Yields . . . . 6 servings.

SURPRISE BAKED BEANS

1   8-ounce can apricots
2   16-ounce cans Beanee Weenees
1/2 cup chopped onion
2 tablespoons brown sugar
1 teaspoon dry mustard

Preheat . . . . . . oven to 350 degrees.
Drain . . . . apricots. Place in large bowl; mash with fork.
Add . . . . Beanee Weenees, onion, brown sugar and dry mustard; mix well.
Spoon . . . . into greased 1 1/2-quart casserole.
Bake . . . . for 1 hour or until bubbly.
Yields . . . . 6 to 8 servings.

✐ **More Yummy Fun**

Pineapple Baked Beans — Substitute crushed pineapple for apricots.

RING-A-LING BEANS

2   10-ounce packages frozen green beans
1   10-ounce can cream of mushroom soup
1 cup water
1   3-ounce can French-fried onion rings
3 slices cheese

Cook . . . . green beans in large saucepan
according to package directions;
drain well.
Add . . . . soup, water and onion rings; mix
well. Place cheese slices on top.
Heat . . . . for 1 minute longer or until cheese
melts.
Yields . . . . 6 servings.

☞ **More Yummy Fun**

Pretty Party Beans — Save several onion rings from
can to place on top cheese slices.

CHEESY BROCCOLI CASSEROLE

2   10-ounce packages frozen chopped broccoli
4 ounces Velveeta cheese
1/4 cup butter
1 stack-pack Ritz crackers, crushed
1/4 cup melted butter

Preheat . . . . . . oven to 350 degrees.
Cook . . . . broccoli according to the package directions; drain well. Place in 8x8-inch baking dish.
Cut . . . . cheese into cubes. Combine with 1/4 cup butter in saucepan over low heat.
Cook . . . . until cheese and butter are melted and well blended, stirring constantly. Spoon over broccoli.
Mix . . . . crumbs with melted butter; sprinkle over broccoli and cheese.
Bake . . . . for 30 minutes or until golden brown.
Yields . . . . 6 servings.

OLD KING COLE SPINACH

2 eggs
2 cups cooked spinach

Preheat . . . . . . oven to 350 degrees.
Beat . . . . eggs in bowl until foamy.
Chop . . . . well-drained spinach finely. Add to
eggs; mix well.
Pour . . . . into buttered 1-quart baking dish.
Bake . . . . for 30 minutes or until set.
Yields . . . . 2 servings.

Garnish with a little shredded carrot, crumbled crisp-fried bacon, pimento strips, chopped hard-boiled eggs or your own favorite garnish.

SURPRISE CARROT LOAF

1 cup ground carrots
1 cup ground peanuts
1 cup bread crumbs
1 tablespoon melted butter
1 cup chopped tomatoes
4 eggs

Preheat . . . . . . oven to 350 degrees.
Put . . . . carrots, peanuts and crumbs through food grinder.
Combine . . . . . carrot mixture with butter and tomatoes in bowl; mix well.
Beat . . . . eggs in small bowl until foamy. Add to carrot mixture; mix well.
Pour . . . . into greased 5x9-inch loaf pan.
Bake . . . . for 1 hour or until set.
Yields . . . . 6 to 8 servings.

FIVE-CUP FRUIT SALAD

1 cup drained mandarin oranges
1 cup drained pineapple tidbits
1 cup coconut
1 cup miniature marshmallows
1 cup sour cream

Combine . . . . . oranges, pineapple, coconut, marshmallows and sour cream in bowl; mix gently.
Cover . . . . with plastic wrap.
Chill . . . . until serving time.
Spoon . . . . into pretty serving bowl.
Yields . . . . 6 to 8 servings.

✏ **More Yummy Fun**

Everybody's Favorite Fruit Salad — Try one or more of the following suggestions for a new and different fruit salad.

1. Substitute fruit cocktail for oranges and pineapple.
2. Use colored marshmallows.
3. Add 1/2 cup chopped pecans.
4. Substitute whipped topping or vanilla yogurt for sour cream.
5. Add 1 cup cottage cheese.

GRANDMA'S POTATO SALAD

2 cups chopped cooked potatoes
2 hard-boiled eggs, chopped
1/3 cup chopped sweet pickles
1/4 cup mayonnaise
1 teaspoon celery seed
1 tablespoon vinegar
1 teaspoon sugar
Salt and pepper to taste

Combine . . . . . potatoes, eggs and pickles in medium bowl.

Combine . . . . . mayonnaise, celery seed, vinegar, sugar and salt and pepper in small bowl; mix well.

Pour . . . . mayonnaise mixture over the potato mixture; mix gently.

Cover . . . . with plastic wrap.

Chill . . . . until serving time.

Yields . . . . 4 servings.

TOSSED SALAD

1 small head lettuce
1/2 cup chopped celery
1/2 cup shredded carrots
1 hard-boiled egg
1 tomato
1/2 cup (about) favorite salad dressing
1/2 cup shredded Cheddar cheese

Wash . . . . lettuce and drain well. Tear or chop into bite-sized pieces and place in salad bowl. Add celery and carrots.
Slice . . . . hard-boiled egg and tomato. Add to salad; toss lightly.
Add . . . . as much salad dressing as you like; toss lightly.
Sprinkle . . . . . . cheese on top. Serve right away.
Yields . . . . 4 servings.

After School

SNACKS

ANTS ON A LOG

Bananas
Peanut butter
Raisins

Slice . . . . bananas in half lengthwise.
Spread . . . . cut sides of bananas generously
with peanut butter.
Sprinkle . . . . . . raisins on peanut butter.
Yields . . . . As many as you want.

This recipe makes a nutritious after-school snack for children as well as adults.

✏ **More Yummy Fun**

Crunchy Logs — Substitute celery sticks for bananas.

Cheesy Stuff — Substitute cream cheese for peanut butter with either bananas or celery.

Nutty Ants — Substitute chopped nuts for raisins with any combination of bananas, celery, cream cheese and peanut butter.

PEANUT BUTTER-STUFFED APPLES

Apples
Peanut butter
Raisins
Granola
Wheat germ
Oats
Honey

Remove . . . . . . cores from apples carefully. Do not cut apples into halves.
Combine . . . . . peanut butter with 1 or more of the remaining ingredients in bowl; mix well.
Spoon . . . . 2 tablespoons peanut butter mixture into apples. Wrap in foil.

These are great for camping. Eat them whole or sliced.

ZAC'S SNACK

1   16-ounce package "M & M's" Chocolate
    Candies
1   16-ounce package raisins
1   16-ounce jar peanuts

Combine . . . . . candies, raisins and peanuts in large
                      bowl.
Mix . . . . with wooden spoon as long as you
                      want to.
Add . . . . a package of sugar snacks or any
                      other favorite cereal.
Store . . . . in tightly covered container.
Yields . . . . Lots.

Mom, Dad and Grandparents will love this too.

MICROWAVE CHEESE AND CHIPS

1 package corn chips
Shredded Cheddar cheese
Shredded mozzarella cheese

Spread . . . . chips on plate.
Sprinkle . . . . . . with one or both kinds of cheese.
Microwave . . . on High for about 1 minute or until cheese melts.
Yields . . . . 4 servings.

COCONUT AND BANANA TREATS

2 bananas
1/4 cup peanut butter
Shredded coconut
Maraschino cherries, sliced

Peel . . . . bananas and cut each in half
lengthwise.
Spread . . . . 2 halves with peanut butter.
Arrange . . . . . . cherries over peanut butter. Top with
remaining banana halves.
Roll . . . . in coconut. Cut into small pieces.
Yields . . . . 2 or 3 servings.

FRUIT GORP

8 ounces prunes
8 ounces dried dates
8 ounces raisins
$1/2$ cup nuts
$1/2$ cup bran

Chop . . . . prunes, dates, raisins and nuts very finely in food processor container or in food grinder.
Combine . . . . . chopped fruit and nuts with bran in bowl; mix well.
Shape . . . . into bars.
Yields . . . . 8 to 10 servings.

HAMBURGER YUM YUMS

Coconut
Green food coloring
Chocolate-covered mint cookies
Vanilla wafers
Honey
Sesame seed

Combine . . . . . coconut with several drops of food coloring in bowl; mix until coconut is tinted green.

Place . . . . coconut on chocolate-covered cookies.

Brush . . . . half the vanilla wafers with honey. Sprinkle with sesame seed.

Place . . . . chocolate-covered cookies on remaining vanilla wafers. Top with sesame seed vanilla wafers.

These look just like miniature hamburgers.

KNOX BLOCKS

3   3-ounce packages flavored gelatin
4 envelopes unflavored gelatin
4 cups boiling water

Combine . . . . . flavored and unflavored gelatin in large bowl.
Add . . . . boiling water very carefully or have Mom help. Stir until gelatin dissolves.
Spray . . . . 9x13-inch dish with nonstick cooking spray.
Pour . . . . gelatin mixture into dish.
Chill . . . . for 2 hours. Cut into squares.
Store . . . . in tightly sealed plastic bags.
Yields . . . . 40 squares.

These are great for school lunches and parties as they don't melt.

PORCUPINE QUILLS

4 ounces Cheddar cheese
1   16-ounce can pineapple chunks, drained
1   8-ounce jar olives
Toothpicks
1 whole grapefruit

Cut . . . . cheese into chunks the size of
pineapple chunks.
Slide . . . . pineapple chunk, olive and cheese
chunks onto toothpicks.
Stick . . . . toothpicks in grapefruit, starting at
bottom and going in a circle until the
whole grapefruit is covered.
Place . . . . porcupine on serving plate.
Yields . . . . 2 dozen.

POPCORN FANTASY

1 cup butter
1   16-ounce package marshmallows
8 cups popped popcorn
1 cup peanuts
1 cup "M & M's" Chocolate Candies
1 cup gumdrops

Heat . . . . butter and marshmallows in saucepan over low heat until melted and well blended, stirring constantly.
Combine . . . . . popcorn, peanuts and candies in bowl; mix lightly.
Pour . . . . marshmallow mixture over popcorn; mix well.
Press . . . . in 9x13-inch dish.
Chill . . . . in refrigerator for several hours.
Cut . . . . into squares.
Yields . . . . 6 dozen.

OUT-OF-THIS-WORLD CHEESY PRETZELS

1½ cups baking mix
½ cup milk
½ cup shredded Cheddar cheese
1 egg, beaten
½ teaspoon salt

Combine . . . . . baking mix, milk and cheese in bowl; mix well.
Roll . . . . into 8x12-inch rectangle on floured surface.
Cut . . . . into 1x8-inch strips.
Twist . . . . each strip into pretzel shape and place on greased baking sheet.
Brush . . . . strips with beaten egg. Sprinkle with salt.
Bake . . . . at 400 degrees for 20 to 25 minutes or until golden brown.
Yields . . . . 1 dozen.

ROASTED PUMPKIN SEED

2 cups pumpkin seed
2 tablespoons butter
1 teaspoon salt

Wash . . . . pumpkin seed in colander. Drain well and pat dry on paper towel.
Sauté . . . . pumpkin seed, butter and salt in large skillet for 3 minutes, stirring constantly with spoon.
Spread . . . . on baking sheet.
Bake . . . . at 250 degrees for 30 minutes or until brown.
Spread . . . . on paper towels to cool.
Yields . . . . 2 cups.

GRANNY RIDDLE'S CRACKERS

2 double graham crackers
Smooth peanut butter
Large marshmallows

Spread . . . . 1 cracker with peanut butter.
Cut . . . . marshmallows in half; place on
remaining cracker.
Place . . . . on baking sheet.
Broil . . . . until marshmallows are brown. Press
crackers together. Break into pieces.
Yields . . . . 1 serving.

MILKANILLA

1 cup milk
1/2 teaspoon sugar
1/8 teaspoon vanilla extract

Combine . . . . . milk, sugar and vanilla in glass.
Mix . . . . well and drink.
Yields . . . . 1 serving.

✎ **More Yummy Fun**

Choose-a-Flavor Milk — There are many different
    flavor extracts that can be substituted for the
    vanilla. Try almond, lemon, orange, raspberry or
    banana, to name just a few.

ORANGE JUBILEE

1¹/₂ cups orange juice
1 pint vanilla ice cream, softened
Fresh orange slices
Maraschino cherries

Combine . . . . . orange juice and ice cream in
medium bowl.
Stir . . . . until smooth.
Pour . . . . into glasses. Decorate glasses with
orange slices and cherries.
Yields . . . . 3 cups.

✐ **More Yummy Fun**

Juicy Jubilee — Use almost any favorite fruit juice in
place of orange juice. Try grape, pineapple or
cranberry or even a combination of juices like
pineapple and orange.

Do-It-Yourself

BREADS

CINNAMON AND RAISIN BISCUITS

2 cups self-rising flour
2 tablespoons sugar
1 teaspoon cream of tartar
5 tablespoons shortening
1 cup buttermilk
Melted butter
2 cups sugar
3 tablespoons cinnamon
1 tablespoon oil
1/4 cup raisins

Preheat . . . . . . oven to 375 degrees.
Combine . . . . . flour, 2 tablespoons sugar and
cream of tartar in bowl.
Cut . . . . shortening into mixture with pastry
blender until mixture is crumbly.
Add . . . . buttermilk; mix until mixture clings
together and forms ball.
Sprinkle . . . . . . a small amount of additional flour
onto counter top. Roll dough into
thin rectangle on floured surface
with rolling pin.
Brush . . . . with melted butter. Mix 2 cups sugar,
cinnamon, oil and raisins in small
bowl. Sprinkle over dough. Roll as
for jelly roll; cut into 1½-inch slices.
Place on greased baking sheet.
Bake . . . . for 15 minutes or until golden brown.
Yields . . . . 6 to 8 servings.

CHOCOLATE CROISSANTS

1   8-count package refrigerator crescent rolls
1/4 cup melted butter
4 fun-sized 3 Musketeer candy bars
1/4 cup confectioners' sugar

Preheat . . . . . . oven to 375 degrees.
Separate . . . . . roll dough. Slice candy bars carefully into halves lengthwise.
Brush . . . . rolls with melted butter. Place candy slice at wide end of each triangle; roll as for jelly roll.
Place . . . . on baking sheet. Brush with butter.
Bake . . . . for 12 minutes or until brown.
Sprinkle . . . . . . the confectioners' sugar lightly over hot croissants.
Serve . . . . hot or cold.
Yields . . . . 8 servings.

✐ **More Yummy Fun**

Candy Bar Croissants — Substitute Milky Way, Snicker or other favorite candy bars for 3 Musketeers.

PBJ Croissants — Substitute peanut butter and favorite jelly for candy bars.

APPLESAUCE SPICE BREAD

1   2-layer package yellow cake mix
1   3-ounce package vanilla instant pudding mix
1/2 teaspoon cinnamon
1/2 teaspoon nutmeg
1 cup applesauce
1/2 cup raisins

Preheat . . . . . . oven to 350 degrees.
Grease . . . . and flour two 5x9-inch loaf pans.
Combine . . . . . cake mix, pudding mix, cinnamon, nutmeg and applesauce in mixer bowl.
Beat . . . . at low speed for 1 minute. Beat at high speed for 4 minutes.
Pour . . . . into prepared loaf pans.
Bake . . . . for 30 to 35 minutes or until you can stick a toothpick in the center and it comes out clean.
Cool . . . . in pans for 15 minutes.
Remove . . . . . . carefully from pans; place on wire racks.
Cool . . . . completely before slicing.
Yields . . . . 2 loaves.

CHILD'S BANANA BREAD

4 ripe bananas
1 egg
1 cup sugar
1½ cups self-rising flour
¼ cup melted butter
½ cup chopped nuts

Preheat . . . . . . oven to 325 degrees.
Grease . . . . 5x9-inch loaf pan.
Mash . . . . bananas with fork on large dinner plate.
Combine . . . . . egg and sugar in bowl; mix well. Add butter and bananas; blend well.
Add . . . . flour; stir until well mixed. Add nuts; mix well.
Pour . . . . into prepared pan.
Bake . . . . for 1 hour.
Yields . . . . 1 loaf.

NUTTY MONKEY BREAD

4   10-count cans refrigerator biscuits
1 1/2 cups sugar
2 tablespoons cinnamon
1 cup chopped nuts
1/4 cup melted butter
3 tablespoons water

Preheat . . . . . . oven to 350 degrees.
Grease . . . . bundt pan.
Cut . . . . each biscuit into 4 pieces.
Combine . . . . . sugar and cinnamon in plastic bag. Add biscuit pieces several at a time; shake bag until biscuits are coated with cinnamon-sugar.
Alternate . . . . . layers of biscuits and nuts in prepared bundt pan.
Combine . . . . . remaining cinnamon-sugar, butter and water in saucepan over medium heat.
Bring . . . . to a boil, stirring constantly. Pour over biscuits in bundt pan.
Bake . . . . for 30 minutes. Place serving plate on top of pan. Turn plate and pan over carefully. Remove pan.
Serve . . . . Monkey Bread hot or cold.
Yields . . . . 20 servings.

GRANDPA GOOSE'S CORN MUFFINS

1 cup cornmeal
1 cup flour
4 teaspoons baking powder
1/4 cup sugar
1/2 teaspoon salt
1 cup milk
1 egg
1/4 cup oil

Preheat . . . . oven to 425 degrees.
Grease . . . . 12 muffin cups.
Combine . . . . . cornmeal, flour, baking powder, sugar and salt in bowl; mix well.
Add . . . . milk, egg and oil; mix well.
Spoon . . . . into greased muffin cups.
Bake . . . . for 15 to 20 minutes or until golden brown.
Serve . . . . muffins hot with butter.
Yields . . . . 12 muffins.

CRANBERRY CORN MUFFINS

1   8-ounce package corn muffin mix
1   7-ounce can jellied cranberry sauce

Preheat ...... oven to 375 degrees.
Grease .... 12 muffin cups.
Prepare ...... corn muffin mix according to the package directions.
Chop .... cranberry sauce into small pieces
Add .... to muffin batter; fold in gently.
Spoon .... enough batter into each muffin cup to fill 2/3 full.
Bake .... for 12 minutes or until golden brown.
Serve .... muffins hot with butter.
Yields .... 12 muffins.

MUFFINS IN A HURRY

2 cups self-rising flour
1 cup milk
1/4 cup mayonnaise

Preheat . . . . . . oven to 400 degrees.
Grease . . . . 12 muffin cups.
Sift . . . . flour into bowl.
Add . . . . milk and salad dressing; stir just until flour is moistened. Batter will be lumpy.
Spoon . . . . enough batter into muffin cups to fill 2/3 full.
Bake . . . . for 20 minutes or until golden brown.
Serve . . . . muffins hot with butter.
Yields . . . . 12 muffins.

QUICK YEAST ROLLS

1 package dry yeast
3/4 cup warm water
2 1/2 cups buttermilk baking mix
1/4 cup melted butter

Dissolve . . . . . . yeast in warm water in large bowl.
Add . . . . baking mix gradually; mix well.
Knead . . . . on floured surface until smooth and elastic.
Let . . . . dough stand for 5 minutes. Pat into rectangle; cut into squares.
Roll . . . . each square in melted butter; place in 9x13-inch baking pan.
Let . . . . rise for 30 minutes or until doubled in bulk.
Preheat . . . . . . oven to 400 degrees.
Bake . . . . for 20 minutes or until golden brown.
Yields . . . . 1 1/2 dozen.

GOODIES

Of All Kinds

ANGELS ON HORSEBACK

8 large graham crackers
4 small milk chocolate candy bars
12 marshmallows

Preheat . . . . . . broiler.
Arrange . . . . . . 4 graham crackers on baking sheet.
Top . . . . each graham cracker with 1 candy bar.
Place . . . . under broiler. Broil until candy is slightly melted.
Remove . . . . from oven. Place 3 marshmallows on chocolate on each cracker.
Broil . . . . until marshmallows are slightly brown and puffed.
Remove . . . . . . from oven. Top with remaining graham crackers.
Serve . . . . warm with glass of cold milk.
Yields . . . . 4 servings.

QUICK BUTTERSCOTCH CRUNCHIES

2 cups butterscotch chips
1/2 cup peanut butter
6 cups cornflakes

Combine . . . . . butterscotch chips and peanut butter in saucepan over low heat.
Heat . . . . until melted, stirring constantly.
Remove . . . . . . from heat.
Add . . . . cornflakes; stir until well mixed.
Drop . . . . by teaspoonfuls onto waxed paper.
Let . . . . stand until cool and firm.
Yields . . . . 3 dozen.

➩ **More Yummy Fun**

Chocolate and Butterscotch Crunchies — Use 1 cup chocolate chips and 1 cup butterscotch chips instead of 2 cups butterscotch chips.

Chocolate and Peanut Crunchies — Use 2 cups chocolate chips instead of butterscotch chips and add 1/2 cup chopped peanuts.

PECAN BUTTERSCOTCH CANDY CRUNCH

Pecans
1 cup butter
1 cup sugar
1 cup butterscotch chips

Line . . . . 10x15-inch baking sheet with foil.
Sprinkle . . . . as many chopped pecans as you want evenly over foil. Set aside.
Melt . . . . butter in 1-quart saucepan over medium heat. Add sugar; mix well.
Cook . . . . for 8 minutes, stirring constantly with wooden spoon. Mixture will be pale caramel color.
Spoon . . . . hot mixture evenly over pecans.
Cool . . . . for 2 minutes. Sprinkle butterscotch chips over top.
Let . . . . stand for 4 to 5 minutes or until the butterscotch chips have melted enough to spread evenly with rubber spatula.
Sprinkle . . . . additional pecans over top.
Chill . . . . for 30 minutes or until firm. Break into small pieces.
Yields . . . . 3 dozen or more.

CINDERELLA CRISPS

6 slices white bread
1   14-ounce can sweetened condensed milk
3 cups flaked coconut

Preheat . . . . oven to 375 degrees.
Trim . . . . crusts from bread. Cut each slice into 4 strips.
Pour . . . . condensed milk into shallow dish.
Dip . . . . each bread piece into condensed milk; roll in coconut to coat.
Place . . . . on greased baking sheet. Do not allow pieces to touch.
Bake . . . . for 8 to 10 minutes or until light brown. Remove to wire rack to cool.
Store . . . . in airtight container.
Yields . . . . 2 dozen.

✐ **More Yummy Fun**

Raisin Crisps — Substitute raisin bread for white bread.

CUPCAKE CONES

1   2-layer package cake mix
1   16-ounce can frosting
24 flat-bottom ice cream cones
Candy sprinkles

Select . . . . your favorite flavor cake mix and frosting go-togethers.

Preheat . . . . oven as directed on the cake mix package.

Prepare . . . . . . cake mix according to the package directions.

Spoon . . . . enough batter into ice cream cones to fill 1/3 full. Arrange cones on baking sheet.

Bake . . . . for 20 to 25 minutes or until cake tests done when toothpick inserted in center of cake comes out clean.

Remove . . . . to wire rack to cool completely.

Spread . . . . each cupcake with frosting; swirl frosting into point at center of top.

Decorate . . . . . with candy sprinkles.

Yields . . . . 2 dozen.

GRAHAM CRACKER FACES

6 graham crackers
1 tablespoon peanut butter
1 tablespoon cream cheese
48 raisins
1/4 cup shredded coconut

Spread . . . . 3 crackers with peanut butter and 3 crackers with cream cheese.

Place . . . . raisins to make eyes, nose and mouth on each cracker.

Sprinkle . . . . . . coconut around face to resemble hair.

Arrange . . . . . . graham cracker faces on serving plate.

Yields . . . . 1/2 dozen.

BANANA PRALINE SUNDAES

3 tablespoons butter
1/3 cup packed brown sugar
1/4 cup golden raisins
2 bananas, sliced
1 pint vanilla ice cream
1/3 cup chopped pecans

Melt . . . . butter in skillet over low heat.
Blend . . . . in brown sugar. Cook for 1 to 2 minutes or until clear and golden, stirring constantly. Add raisins and bananas.
Cook . . . . for 5 minutes or until hot, stirring several times.
Scoop . . . . ice cream into dessert dishes. Spoon hot banana mixture over ice cream.
Sprinkle . . . . pecans over top. Serve immediately.
Yields . . . . 4 servings.

CLOWN FACE SUNDAE

1 scoop vanilla ice cream
1 ice cream cone
Chocolate chips
1 maraschino cherry
3 or 4 ice cream wafers

Place . . . . ice cream in center of serving dish.
Press . . . . cone onto ice cream to resemble hat.
Add . . . . chocolate chips for eyes and mouth and cherry for nose.
Cut . . . . ice cream wafers into triangles. Press points of triangles into base of ice cream scoop to resemble collar.
Yields . . . . 1 clown sundae.

✏ More Yummy Fun

Any-Flavor Clown — Substitute your favorite ice cream flavor for vanilla.

ROCKY ROAD PARFAITS

1   4-ounce package chocolate instant
    pudding mix
2 cups milk
1/2 cup marshmallow creme
2 tablespoons chopped almonds

Prepare . . . . . . pudding mix with milk according to
the package directions.

Let . . . . pudding stand at room temperature
for several minutes or until slightly
thickened.

Spoon . . . . about 1/3 of the pudding into 4 parfait
glasses. Add about 1/3 of the
marshmallow creme.

Repeat . . . . pudding and marshmallow creme
layers 2 more times.

Sprinkle . . . . . . almonds over top.

Chill . . . . for 30 minutes or longer.

Yields . . . . 4 servings.

MISSY'S CANDY ORNAMENTS

Hard candies with flowers in the centers
Plain hard candies

Preheat . . . . . . oven to 300 degrees.
Line . . . . baking sheet with foil.
Arrange . . . . . . several hard candies on baking sheet. Leave space between the candies to allow for spreading.
Bake . . . . for 10 minutes.
Let . . . . candies cool on baking sheet for several minutes. Make hole in each candy near edge with nut pick or point of pencil.
Insert . . . . hangers through holes. Hang the ornaments on the Christmas tree or wherever you like.
Yields . . . . as many as you like.

The ornaments are edible or may be stored for another time.

UNBAKED CRISPIE GOODIES

½ cup light corn syrup
½ cup peanut butter
3 cups Rice Krispies

Cover . . . . tray or cookie sheet with waxed
paper.
Combine . . . . . corn syrup and peanut butter in
medium bowl; mix until well blended.
Add . . . . Rice Krispies; mix well.
Drop . . . . mixture by teaspoonfuls onto waxed
paper-lined tray.
Let . . . . stand for several minutes or until
firm.
Eat . . . . immediately or store between layers
of waxed paper in airtight container.
Yields . . . . 3 to 4 dozen.

CHOCOLATE-COVERED PEANUTS

1 cup semisweet chocolate chips
1 teaspoon peanut butter
1 cup Spanish peanuts

Melt . . . . chocolate chips in microwave in glass casserole or in saucepan over low heat. Stir several times while chocolate melts.

Blend . . . . in peanut butter.

Add . . . . peanuts; stir until peanuts are coated with chocolate.

Drop . . . . by teaspoonfuls onto waxed paper.

Let . . . . stand for several minutes or until chocolate is firm.

Yields . . . . 3 dozen.

CHOCOLATE SPIDERS

1½ cups semisweet chocolate chips
1   5-ounce can chow mein noodles
1 cup salted peanuts

Place . . . . chocolate chips in top of double
boiler over water.
Bring . . . . water to a boil; reduce heat to low.
Heat . . . . until chocolate melts, stirring
occasionally.
Add . . . . noodles and peanuts; mix well.
Drop . . . . by teaspoonfuls onto greased tray
or cookie sheet.
Chill . . . . in refrigerator for 8 hours to
overnight.
Yields . . . . 3 dozen.

EDIBLE PLAYDOUGH

1 cup peanut butter
1 cup corn syrup
1¼ cups confectioners' sugar
1¼ cups dry milk powder

Combine . . . . . . peanut butter and corn syrup in large bowl; mix until smooth.

Mix . . . . confectioners' sugar and dry milk powder in small bowl.

Add . . . . confectioners' sugar mixture to peanut butter mixture; mix well. May add enough additional confectioners' sugar to make of consistency of play dough.

Let . . . . kids create yummy sculptures and then gobble them up.

Yields . . . . 2½ to 3 cups.

MICROWAVE FANTASY FUDGE

3/4 cup margarine
3 cups sugar
1   5-ounce can evaporated milk
2 cups semisweet chocolate chips
1   7-ounce jar marshmallow creme
1 teaspoon vanilla extract

Microwave . . . . margarine in 4-quart bowl on High until melted.

Add . . . . sugar and evaporated milk; mix well.

Microwave . . . . on High for 5 minutes or until the mixture comes to a boil, stirring after 3 minutes. Mix well and scrape side of bowl.

Microwave . . . . for 5$\frac{1}{2}$ minutes longer, stirring after 3 minutes.

Add . . . . chocolate chips; stir until melted. Add marshmallow creme and vanilla; blend well.

Pour . . . . into greased 9x13-inch pan. Let stand until completely cool.

Cut . . . . into squares.

Yields . . . . 3 pounds.

EASY FUDGE

1 pound confectioners' sugar
1/2 cup baking cocoa
1/4 cup milk
1 stick margarine
Pinch of salt
1 teaspoon vanilla extract
1/2 cup chopped nuts

Combine . . . . . confectioners' sugar, cocoa and milk in large glass bowl.
Cut . . . . margarine into 4 portions. Add to bowl.
Microwave . . . on High for about 2 minutes or until margarine is melted. Mix until smooth.
Add . . . . vanilla and nuts; mix well.
Pour . . . . into greased dish; spread evenly.
Let . . . . stand for 20 to 30 minutes or until cool and firm.
Cut . . . . into squares.
Yields . . . . 1 1/2 pounds.

CRISPIE PEANUT BUTTER BARS

1 cup semisweet chocolate chips
$^1/_3$ cup peanut butter
4 cups Cocoa Krispies

Combine . . . . . . chocolate chips and peanut butter in
saucepan over low heat.
Heat . . . . until chocolate chips are melted and
the mixture is well blended, stirring
constantly; remove from heat.
Add . . . . cereal; stir until well mixed.
Pat . . . . into greased 9x9-inch pan.
Chill . . . . until firm. Cut into bars.
Yields . . . . 3 dozen.

✎ **More Yummy Fun**

Not-So-Chocolate Crispie Bars — Substitute Rice
Krispies for Cocoa Krispies.

Scotchy Bars — Substitute butterscotch chips for
chocolate chips.

COCONUT SNOWBALLS

1 1/3 cups coconut
Food coloring
1/2 teaspoon milk
1 quart favorite ice cream

Place . . . . coconut in bowl.
Mix . . . . several drops of any desired food coloring with milk.
Sprinkle . . . . food coloring mixture over coconut; toss with fork until coconut is tinted evenly.
Scoop . . . . ice cream into balls. Roll each ice cream ball in tinted coconut until coated.
Place . . . . ice cream balls in dessert dishes to serve right away.
May . . . . place ice cream balls in 9x13-inch pan, cover tightly and store in freezer until ready to serve.
Yields . . . . 8 to 10 servings.

PEANUT BUTTER CUPS

1 roll refrigerator peanut butter cookie dough
36 miniature peanut butter cups

Preheat . . . . oven to 375 degrees.
Slice . . . . cookie dough into 1-inch slices; cut each slice into 4 pieces.
Place . . . . cookie dough pieces in miniature muffin cups.
Bake . . . . for 10 minutes or until golden brown.
Unwrap . . . . peanut butter cups; press 1 cup into each warm cookie.
Cool . . . . completely before removing from muffin cups.
Yields . . . . 3 dozen.

PEANUT BUTTER CANDY

1/3 cup light corn syrup
1/3 cup peanut butter
1/2 cup dry milk powder
1/3 cup confectioners' sugar

Combine . . . . . . corn syrup and peanut butter in
bowl; mix with spoon until well
blended.
Add . . . . dry milk powder and confectioners'
sugar; mix well.
Shape . . . . into log. Wrap in plastic wrap.
Store . . . . in refrigerator until ready to serve.
Cut . . . . into slices; arrange on serving plate.
Yields . . . . 1 dozen.

PEANUT BUTTER KISSES

1 cup creamy peanut butter
3/4 cup packed light brown sugar
1 egg
1 teaspoon vanilla extract
1/4 cup semisweet chocolate chips

Preheat . . . . oven to 300 degrees.

Combine . . . . . . peanut butter, brown sugar, egg and vanilla in medium bowl; mix with spoon until smooth.

Shape . . . . into 3/4-inch diameter balls; place 1-inch apart on ungreased cookie sheet.

Flatten . . . . slightly and place 1 chocolate chip in center of each cookie.

Bake . . . . for 20 minutes or until light brown.

Cool . . . . on cookie sheet for 1 minute.

Remove . . . . cookies from cookie sheet to wire rack to cool completely.

Yields . . . . 4 dozen.

BEST BANANA SHAKE

2 bananas, cut up
$1/3$ cup lemon juice
1 cup water
1   14-ounce can sweetened condensed milk
2 cups crushed ice

Combine . . . . . bananas, lemon juice, water and condensed milk in blender container.
Place . . . . cover on container.
Process . . . . . . until smooth.
Add . . . . ice. Place cover on container.
Process . . . . . . until smooth and creamy.
Pour . . . . into chilled glasses. Garnish with bite-sized pieces of your favorite fresh fruit.
Store . . . . prepared shake in refrigerator. It will stay thick and tasty.
Yields . . . . 6 servings.

STRAWBERRY MILK SHAKE

2 scoops strawberry ice cream
2 cups milk

Place . . . . 2 scoops strawberry ice cream in tall glass.
Let . . . . stand for several minutes or until slightly softened.
Add . . . . milk; stir until smooth and creamy.
Garnish . . . . . . with 1 or 2 fresh strawberries.
Yields . . . . 1 serving.

✎ **More Yummy Fun**

Milk Shake Mix-Up — Use other favorite flavor ice cream or even 1 scoop of 2 different flavors.

HOLIDAY PUNCH

6 liters ginger ale
1 gallon lime sherbet

Chill . . . . ginger ale in refrigerator for several hours.
Let . . . . sherbet stand at room temperature for several minutes to soften.
Spoon . . . . sherbet into punch bowl.
Pour . . . . the ginger ale slowly over the sherbet, stirring gently.
Ladle . . . . punch into punch cups.
Serve . . . . immediately.
Yields . . . . 2½ gallons punch.

✏ **More Yummy Fun**

Anytime Punch — Use any favorite flavor sherbet with ginger ale or substitute lemon-lime soda for ginger ale.

Pretty Punch Bowl — Add several slices of lemon, lime, strawberries or other fruit to the punch bowl for a colorful garnish.

PEPPERMINT FLOAT

1 quart peppermint ice cream
2 tablespoons finely crushed peppermint candy
4 cups milk

Place . . . . 2 cups ice cream in large mixer
bowl. Let stand for several minutes
to soften slightly.
Add . . . . peppermint candy and milk.
Beat . . . . with electric mixer at low speed until
thick and slushy.
Pour . . . . into chilled glasses.
Scoop . . . . remaining ice cream into balls.
Place . . . . 1 scoop carefully in each glass.
Yields . . . . 6 servings.

✎ **More Yummy Fun**

Toffee Crunch Float — Substitute crushed chocolate-
covered toffee bars for peppermint candy.

Happy Ending

DESSERTS

P. J.'S APPLE SQUARES

1/2 cup packed brown sugar
1/2 cup sugar
1 egg
1/4 cup melted margarine
1 cup flour
1 teaspoon baking powder
1/4 teaspoon salt
1/4 teaspoon cinnamon
1 teaspoon vanilla extract
1/2 cup chopped peeled apple
1/2 cup sugar
1 1/2 teaspoons cinnamon

Preheat . . . . . . oven to 350 degrees.
Combine . . . . . brown sugar, 1/2 cup sugar, egg and margarine in bowl; mix well.
Mix . . . . flour, baking powder, salt and 1/4 teaspoon cinnamon.
Add . . . . flour mixture to sugar mixture; mix well.
Stir . . . . in vanilla and apples. Spoon into greased 9-inch baking pan.
Combine . . . . . remaining 1/2 cup sugar and 1 1/2 teaspoons cinnamon in small bowl. Sprinkle over batter.
Bake . . . . for 30 minutes.
Yields . . . . 12 squares.

ICE CREAM BANANA PUDDINGS

1   4-ounce package vanilla instant pudding mix
2 cups milk
1   12-ounce package vanilla wafers
3 or 4 bananas, thinly sliced
1 pint vanilla ice cream
1   8-ounce container whipped topping

Prepare . . . . the pudding mix with the milk using
the package directions.
Place . . . . several vanilla wafers in the bottom
and around edge of 6 dessert dishes.
Spoon . . . . pudding into dishes.
Add . . . . layer of bananas and 1 scoop ice
cream to each dish.
Top . . . . with whipped topping.
Yields . . . . 6 servings.

CHERRY PIZZA DESSERT

2 cans cherry pie filling
1   2-layer package white cake mix
1 stick margarine, sliced
1/2 cup chopped pecans

Preheat . . . . . . oven to 350 degrees.
Pour . . . . pie filling into 9x11-inch baking pan.
Sprinkle . . . . . . dry cake mix over pie filling.
Dot . . . . butter over cake mix. Sprinkle pecans over butter. Do not stir.
Bake . . . . for 30 minutes or until brown.
Yields . . . . 6 to 8 servings.

✎ More Yummy Fun

Apple Pizza Dessert — Substitute apple pie filling for cherry and sprinkle 1/2 teaspoon cinnamon over cake mix layer.

CINDERELLA CAKE

1 cup sugar
1/4 cup butter, softened
2 eggs, beaten
1/2 cup milk
1 1/2 cups flour
2 teaspoons baking powder
1 teaspoon vanilla extract

Preheat . . . . oven to 350 degrees.
Cream . . . . sugar and butter in mixer bowl until light and fluffy.
Add . . . . eggs and milk; mix well.
Sift . . . . flour and baking powder together.
Add . . . . to creamed mixture; mix well. Blend in vanilla.
Pour . . . . into greased and floured 9-inch cake pan.
Bake . . . . for 45 minutes or until cake tests done.
Cool . . . . in pan for 5 minutes. Remove to wire rack to cool completely.
Frost . . . . with favorite frosting.
Yields . . . . 8 servings.

CHERRY CHOCOLATE CAKE

1   2-layer package chocolate fudge cake mix
1 can cherry pie filling
2 eggs, beaten
1 teaspoon almond extract
1   16-ounce can chocolate frosting

Preheat . . . . . . oven to 350 degrees.
Combine . . . . . the cake mix, pie filling, eggs and almond extract in large bowl; mix well.
Pour . . . . into greased 9x13-inch cake pan.
Bake . . . . for 30 minutes.
Cool . . . . cake in pan.
Frost . . . . with chocolate frosting.
Cut . . . . into squares.
Yields . . . . 12 servings.

DADDY'S CAKE

1 16-ounce package frozen rolls
1 3-ounce package butterscotch pudding mix
3/4 cup packed brown sugar
1 stick margarine, sliced
1/2 cup chopped nuts

Place . . . . frozen rolls in greased tube pan.
Sprinkle . . . . . . dry pudding mix and brown sugar over rolls.
Place . . . . margarine on top of sugar. Sprinkle with nuts.
Cover . . . . with cloth. Let stand at room temperature overnight.
Preheat . . . . . . oven to 350 degrees.
Bake . . . . for 25 to 30 minutes or until brown.
Cool . . . . in pan for 5 minutes.
Place . . . . serving plate on top of pan; turn plate and pan upside down carefully. Remove pan.
Yields . . . . 12 servings.

HOT FUDGE PUDDING CAKE

3/4 cup sugar
1 cup flour
3 tablespoons baking cocoa
2 teaspoons baking powder
1/4 teaspoon salt
1/2 cup milk
1/3 cup melted butter
1 1/2 teaspoons vanilla extract
1/2 cup sugar
1/2 cup packed brown sugar
1/4 cup baking cocoa
1 1/4 cups hot water

Preheat . . . . . . oven to 350 degrees.
Combine . . . . . 3/4 cup sugar, flour, 3 tablespoons cocoa, baking powder and salt in bowl.
Blend . . . . in milk, butter and vanilla; mix well. Pour into 9x9-inch cake pan.
Mix . . . . remaining 1/2 cup sugar, brown sugar and 1/4 cup cocoa in small bowl. Sprinkle evenly over batter.
Pour . . . . hot water over top; do not stir.
Bake . . . . for 40 minutes or until the center is almost set.
Cool . . . . in pan for 15 minutes.
Spoon . . . . cake into dessert dishes; spoon sauce from bottom of pan over cake.
Yields . . . . 8 to 10 servings.

PINK STUFF

2 16-ounce cans pineapple chunks
1 6-ounce package strawberry gelatin
1 16-ounce container whipped topping

Drain . . . . pineapple, reserving juice.
Add . . . . enough water to reserved juice to measure 3 cups.
Pour . . . . juice mixture into saucepan. Bring to a boil.
Stir . . . . in gelatin until dissolved. Pour into bowl.
Chill . . . . until gelatin is partially set.
Fold . . . . whipped topping and pineapple chunks into gelatin.
Chill . . . . until gelatin is set.
Yields . . . . 12 servings.

DELICIOUS STRAWBERRY DESSERT

1   6-ounce package strawberry gelatin
1   6-ounce package vanilla instant pudding mix
5 cups boiling water
1   8-ounce container whipped topping
2 cups sliced strawberries

Combine . . . . . gelatin and pudding mix in large bowl.
Add . . . . boiling water gradually. Stir until gelatin dissolves.
Chill . . . . until gelatin is partially set.
Fold . . . . in whipped topping and strawberries. Spoon into dessert dishes.
Chill . . . . for several hours or until firm.
Yields . . . . 8 servings.

RAINBOW DESSERT

2 cups boiling water
1   3-ounce package raspberry gelatin
2 bananas, sliced
2 oranges, chopped
3 slices canned pineapple
1 cup whipped cream

Combine . . . . . boiling water and gelatin in bowl. Stir until gelatin dissolves.
Add . . . . fruit to gelatin; mix gently.
Pour . . . . into mold. Cool.
Chill . . . . for several hours or until very firm.
Unmold . . . . . . onto serving plate. Ask your mother how to do this.
Serve . . . . with whipped cream.
Yields . . . . 4 servings.

CHOCOLATE MARSHMALLOW RICE

4 cups uncooked rice
10 chocolate candy bars
1   10-ounce package miniature marshmallows

Prepare . . . . the rice using the package directions
but do not add the salt.
Spread . . . . rice in 10x15-inch buttered dish.
Melt . . . . chocolate bars in double boiler over
hot water.
Stir . . . . in marshmallows. Pour over rice.
Chill . . . . until chocolate is set. Cut into
squares.
Yields . . . . 16 servings.

VANILLA WAFER DESSERT

2   3-ounce packages vanilla instant
    pudding mix
4 cups milk
1   12-ounce container whipped topping
1 can blueberry pie filling
1 cup crushed vanilla wafers

Prepare . . . . . . the pudding mix with the milk using
the package directions.
Fold . . . . whipped topping into pudding.
Spoon . . . . into 9x13-inch dish.
Spread . . . . pie filling over pudding.
Sprinkle . . . . . . vanilla wafer crumbs over pie filling.
Chill . . . . in refrigerator until serving time.
Yields . . . . 12 servings.

BASIC ROLLED COOKIE

³/₄ cup margarine, softened
1 cup sugar
2 eggs
1 teaspoon vanilla extract
2¹/₂ cups flour

Cream . . . . margarine and sugar in bowl until light and fluffy.
Add . . . . eggs and vanilla; mix well.
Stir . . . . in flour. Shape into ball and wrap in plastic wrap.
Chill . . . . for 1 hour or longer.
Preheat . . . . . . oven to 400 degrees.
Roll . . . . on floured surface until thin. Cut with favorite cookie cutters. Place on cookie sheet.
Bake . . . . at 400 degrees for 6 to 8 minutes or until light brown.
Cool . . . . on cookie sheet for 1 minute.
Remove . . . . . . to wire rack to cool completely.
Yields . . . . 2 dozen.

JAMIE'S CHOCOLATE CHIP COOKIES

1/2 cup butter
1/2 cup packed brown sugar
1/2 cup sugar
1 egg, beaten
1 teaspoon vanilla extract
1 cup plus 2 tablespoons flour
1/2 teaspoon soda
1/4 teaspoon salt
1 cup chocolate chips

Melt . . . . butter in saucepan. Add sugars; mix well. Cool.
Add . . . . mixture of egg and vanilla; mix well.
Mix . . . . flour, soda and salt together in bowl. Add butter mixture; mix well.
Stir . . . . in chocolate chips.
Chill . . . . for 1 hour.
Preheat . . . . oven to 375 degrees.
Shape . . . . dough into small balls. Place on cookie sheet.
Bake . . . . for 12 minutes. Do not overbake.
Cool . . . . on cookie sheet for 1 minute.
Remove . . . . to wire rack to cool completely.
Yields . . . . 2 dozen.

DOUBLE CHOCOLATE CHIP COOKIES

1 2-layer package devil's food cake mix
2 eggs
$\frac{1}{2}$ cup oil
1 cup chocolate chips

Preheat . . . . . . oven to 350 degrees.
Combine . . . . . cake mix, eggs and oil in bowl; mix well.
Add . . . . chocolate chips.
Drop . . . . by teaspoonfuls onto cookie sheet.
Bake . . . . for 10 to 12 minutes or until light brown.
Cool . . . . on cookie sheet for 1 minute. Remove cookies to wire rack to cool completely.
Yields . . . . 4 dozen.

✏ **More Yummy Fun**

Mix and Match Cookies — Substitute different flavored cake mixes for chocolate and other add-ins for chocolate chips. Try any of the following combinations.

1. Yellow cake mix and butterscotch chips.
2. Chocolate chip cake mix and chocolate chips.
3. Orange or lemon cake mix and chopped candy orange slices.

NO-BAKE FUDGE COOKIES

1/4 cup butter
2 cups sugar
1/2 cup milk
1/4 cup baking cocoa
Pinch of salt
1 teaspoon vanilla extract
1/2 cup peanut butter
3 cups quick-cooking oats

Melt . . . . butter in saucepan over low heat.
Add . . . . sugar, milk, cocoa and salt; mix well.
Bring . . . . just to the boiling point. Do not boil. Remove from heat.
Add . . . . vanilla, peanut butter and oats; mix well.
Drop . . . . by spoonfuls onto cookie sheet.
Let . . . . stand until firm.
Yields . . . . 3 dozen.

DISGUSTINGLY RICH BROWNIES

1 cup butter
3/4 cup baking cocoa
2 cups sugar
4 eggs, beaten
1 teaspoon vanilla extract
1 1/4 cups flour
1/4 teaspoon salt
1/2 cup chopped walnuts

Preheat . . . . . . oven to 350 degrees.
Melt . . . . butter in saucepan over low heat.
Combine . . . . . . cocoa and sugar in bowl. Add butter; mix well.
Blend . . . . eggs and vanilla. Add to chocolate mixture; mix well.
Stir . . . . in flour, salt and walnuts.
Spoon . . . . into greased 9-inch baking pan; spread evenly.
Bake . . . . for 40 to 50 minutes or until toothpick inserted in center comes out clean.
Cool . . . . in pan. Cut into squares.
Yields . . . . 12 to 16 servings.

FUDGE BROWNIES

1/2 cup butter or margarine
2 ounces unsweetened chocolate
1 cup sugar
2 eggs
1 teaspoon vanilla extract
3/4 cup sifted flour
1/2 cup chopped walnuts

Preheat . . . . oven to 350 degrees
Melt . . . . butter and chocolate in medium
saucepan. Remove from heat.
Stir . . . . in sugar.
Add . . . . eggs 1 at a time, mixing well after
each addition. Blend in vanilla.
Stir . . . . in flour and walnuts.
Spread . . . . in greased 8-inch baking pan.
Bake . . . . for 30 minutes. Cool.
Cut . . . . into squares.
Yields . . . . 16 brownies.

MACAROONS

1/3 cup sugar
3 tablespoons flour
1/8 teaspoon salt
1 1/3 cups coconut
2 egg whites
1/2 teaspoon almond extract
12 candied cherry halves

Preheat . . . . . . oven to 325 degrees.
Combine . . . . . sugar, flour, salt and coconut in bowl.
Add . . . . egg whites and almond extract; mix well.
Drop . . . . by teaspoonfuls onto lightly greased cookie sheet. Place cherry half in center of each cookie.
Bake . . . . for 20 minutes or until edges are light brown.
Remove . . . . . . from baking sheet immediately.
Yields . . . . 1 dozen.

ORANGE BALLS

1   6-ounce can frozen orange juice
    concentrate, thawed
1/2 cup melted margarine
1 pound confectioners' sugar
1   12-ounce package vanilla wafers
2 cups (or more) flaked coconut

Combine . . . . . . orange juice concentrate, margarine
and confectioners' sugar in bowl;
blend well.
Crush . . . . vanilla wafers finely. Add to orange
juice mixture.
Shape . . . . into small balls.
Roll . . . . in coconut to coat. Place on waxed
paper.
Let . . . . stand until firm.
Store . . . . in airtight container in refrigerator.
Yields . . . . 2 to 3 dozen.

PEANUT BUTTER COOKIES

1   2-layer package yellow cake mix
1/2 cup peanut butter
1/2 cup oil
2 eggs

Preheat . . . . . . oven to 350 degrees.
Combine . . . . . dry cake mix, peanut butter, oil and eggs in large bowl; mix well.
Drop . . . . by teaspoonfuls 3 inches apart onto lightly greased cookie sheet.
Press . . . . with fork dipped in water or flour to flatten cookie and to make crisscross pattern.
Bake . . . . for 8 to 10 minutes or until golden brown.
Cool . . . . on cookie sheet for 1 to 2 minutes. Remove cookies to wire rack to cool completely.
Yields . . . . 4 dozen.

SEVEN-LAYER COOKIES

1/2 cup melted margarine
1 cup graham cracker crumbs
1 cup flaked coconut
1   14-ounce can sweetened condensed milk
1 cup semisweet chocolate chips
1 cup butterscotch chips
1 cup pecans

Preheat . . . . . . oven to 350 degrees.
Pour . . . . margarine into 9x13-inch baking pan.
Pat . . . . cracker crumbs evenly into pan.
Sprinkle . . . . . . coconut over crumbs.
Drizzle . . . . condensed milk evenly over coconut.
Sprinkle . . . . . . chocolate chips, butterscotch chips
and pecans over top.
Bake . . . . for 35 minutes.
Cool . . . . completely.
Cut . . . . into squares.
Yields . . . . 2 dozen.

WAYNE'S SNOWBALLS

1 cup butter, softened
1/4 cup sugar
1 cup ground nuts
2 cups flour
Confectioners' sugar

Preheat . . . . oven to 300 degrees.
Cream . . . . butter in mixer bowl until light and fluffy.
Add . . . . sugar, nuts and flour; mix well.
Shape . . . . by tablespoonfuls into balls; place on ungreased cookie sheet.
Bake . . . . for 10 to 15 minutes or until light brown.
Place . . . . 1 cup or more confectioners' sugar in small bowl.
Add . . . . hot cookies 1 at a time; roll in confectioners' sugar until coated. Place on wire rack to cool.
Roll . . . . cooled cookies in confectioner's sugar again. Add extra confectioners' sugar to bowl as necessary.
Yields . . . . 4 dozen.

NO-CRUST FUDGE PIE

2 squares unsweetened chocolate
1/2 cup margarine
2 eggs
1 cup sugar
2 tablespoons self-rising flour
1 teaspoon vanilla extract
1/2 cup pecans

Combine . . . . . . chocolate and margarine in saucepan over low heat.
Heat . . . . just until melted, stirring constantly; remove from heat.
Beat . . . . eggs in small bowl with fork. Add sugar, flour and vanilla; mix well.
Add . . . . chocolate; mix well. Stir in pecans.
Pour . . . . into pie plate greased with a little soft margarine.
Place . . . . pie plate in cold oven.
Turn . . . . on oven to 350 degrees.
Bake . . . . for 30 minutes.
Serve . . . . warm or cold, plain or with ice cream.
Yields . . . . 6 servings.

FLUFFY LEMONADE PIE

1   6-ounce can frozen lemonade concentrate,
    thawed
1   14-ounce can sweetened condensed milk
2 drops of yellow food coloring
1   9-ounce carton whipped topping
1   9-inch graham cracker pie shell

Combine . . . . . lemonade concentrate, sweetened
                condensed milk and food coloring in
                medium bowl; stir until well blended.
Fold . . . . in whipped topping gently.
Pour . . . . into pie shell.
Chill . . . . in refrigerator until serving time.
Yields . . . . 6 servings.

➥ **More Yummy Fun**

Fluffy Limeade Pie — Substitute frozen limeade
        concentrate for lemonade. Tint with 1 drop of
        green food coloring.

FROZEN MILLIONAIRE PIE

1   14-ounce can sweetened condensed milk
1/3 cup lemon juice
1/2 cup drained crushed pineapple
1/2 cup chopped maraschino cherries
1/2 cup chopped pecans
1   8-ounce container whipped topping
1   9-inch graham cracker pie shell

Combine . . . . . . sweetened condensed milk and lemon juice in bowl; blend well.
Add . . . . pineapple, cherries and pecans; mix well.
Fold . . . . in whipped topping gently.
Spoon . . . . into pie shell; smooth top. Cover with plastic wrap.
Freeze . . . . until firm.
Thaw . . . . for 10 minutes before cutting.
Yields . . . . 6 servings.

MILE-HIGH STRAWBERRY PIE

1   10-ounce package frozen strawberries,
  thawed
1 cup sugar
2 egg whites
1 tablespoon lemon juice
1   8-ounce carton whipped topping
1 baked 10-inch deep-dish pie shell

Combine . . . . . strawberries, sugar, egg whites and
lemon juice in mixer bowl.
Beat . . . . with electric mixer at medium speed
for 15 minutes or until stiff peaks
form.
Fold . . . . in whipped topping gently.
Spoon . . . . into pie shell.
Freeze . . . . until firm.
Yields . . . . 8 servings.

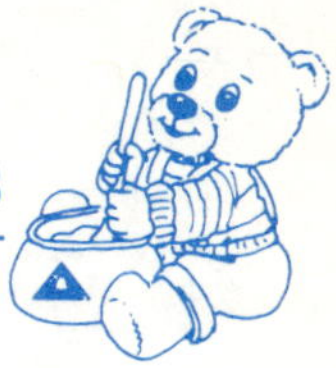

SUBSTITUTION CHART

	Instead of:	Use:
Baking	1 teaspoon baking powder	$\frac{1}{4}$ teaspoon soda plus $\frac{1}{2}$ teaspoon cream of tartar
	1 tablespoon cornstarch (for thickening)	2 tablespoons flour or 1 tablespoon tapioca
	1 cup sifted all-purpose flour	1 cup plus 2 tablespoons sifted cake flour
	1 cup sifted cake flour	1 cup minus 2 tablespoons sifted all-purpose flour
	1 cup fine dry bread crumbs	$\frac{3}{4}$ cup fine cracker crumbs
Dairy	1 cup buttermilk	1 cup sour milk or 1 cup yogurt
	1 cup heavy cream	$\frac{3}{4}$ cup skim milk plus $\frac{1}{3}$ cup butter
	1 cup light cream	$\frac{7}{8}$ cup skim milk plus 3 tablespoons butter
	1 cup sour cream	$\frac{7}{8}$ cup sour milk plus 3 tablespoons butter
	1 cup sour milk	1 cup milk plus 1 tablespoon vinegar or lemon juice or 1 cup buttermilk
Seasoning	1 teaspoon allspice	$\frac{1}{2}$ teaspoon cinnamon plus $\frac{1}{8}$ teaspoon cloves
	1 cup catsup	1 cup tomato sauce plus $\frac{1}{2}$ cup sugar plus 2 tablespoons vinegar
	1 clove of garlic	$\frac{1}{8}$ teaspoon garlic powder or $\frac{1}{8}$ teaspoon instant minced garlic or $\frac{3}{4}$ teaspoon garlic salt
	1 teaspoon Italian spice	$\frac{1}{4}$ teaspoon each oregano, basil, thyme, rosemary plus dash of cayenne
	1 teaspoon lemon juice	$\frac{1}{2}$ teaspoon vinegar
	1 tablespoon mustard	1 teaspoon dry mustard
	1 medium onion	1 tablespoon dried minced onion
Sweet	1 1-ounce square chocolate	$\frac{1}{4}$ cup cocoa plus 1 teaspoon shortening
	$1\frac{2}{3}$ ounces semisweet chocolate	1 ounce unsweetened chocolate plus 4 teaspoons granulated sugar
	1 cup honey	1 to $1\frac{1}{4}$ cups sugar plus $\frac{1}{4}$ cup liquid
	1 cup granulated sugar	1 cup packed brown sugar or 1 cup corn syrup, molasses or honey minus $\frac{1}{4}$ cup liquid

EQUIVALENT CHART

	When the recipe calls for:	Use:
Baking Essentials	½ cup butter	1 stick
	2 cups butter	1 pound
	4 cups all-purpose flour	1 pound
	4½ to 5 cups sifted cake flour	1 pound
	1 square chocolate	1 ounce
	1 cup semisweet chocolate pieces	1 6-ounce package
	4 cups marshmallows	1 pound
	2¼ cups packed brown sugar	1 pound
	4 cups confectioners' sugar	1 pound
	2 cups granulated sugar	1 pound
Cereal & Bread	1 cup fine dry bread crumbs	4 to 5 slices
	1 cup soft bread crumbs	2 slices
	1 cup small bread cubes	2 slices
	1 cup fine cracker crumbs	28 saltines
	1 cup fine graham cracker crumbs	15 crackers
	1 cup vanilla wafer crumbs	22 wafers
	1 cup crushed cornflakes	3 cups uncrushed
	4 cups cooked macaroni	1 8-ounce package
	3½ cups cooked rice	1 cup uncooked
Dairy	1 cup freshly grated cheese	¼ pound
	1 cup cottage cheese	1 8-ounce carton
	1 cup sour cream	1 8-ounce carton
	1 cup whipped cream	½ cup heavy cream
	⅔ cup evaporated milk	1 small can
	1⅔ cups evaporated milk	1 13-ounce can
Fruit	4 cups sliced or chopped apples	4 medium
	1 cup mashed banana	3 medium
	2 cups pitted cherries	4 cups unpitted
	3 cups shredded coconut	½ pound
	4 cups cranberries	1 pound
	1 cup pitted dates	1 8-ounce package
	1 cup candied fruit	1 8-ounce package
	3 to 4 tablespoons lemon juice plus 1 teaspoon grated rind	1 lemon
	⅓ cup orange juice plus 2 teaspoons grated rind	1 orange
	4 cups sliced peaches	8 medium
	2 cups pitted prunes	1 12-ounce package
	3 cups raisins	1 15-ounce package

	When the recipe calls for:	**Use:**
Meats	4 cups chopped cooked chicken 3 cups chopped cooked meat 2 cups cooked ground meat	1 5-pound chicken 1 pound, cooked 1 pound, cooked
Nuts	1 cup chopped nuts	4 ounces, shelled 1 pound, unshelled
Vegetables	2 cups cooked green beans 2½ cups lima beans or red beans 4 cups shredded cabbage 1 cup grated carrots 1 4-ounce can mushrooms 1 cup chopped onion 4 cups sliced or chopped raw potatoes 2 cups canned tomatoes	½ pound fresh or 1 16-ounce can 1 cup dried, cooked 1 pound 1 large ½ pound, fresh 1 large 4 medium 1 16-ounce can

Measurement Equivalents

1 tablespoon = 3 teaspoons
2 tablespoons = 1 ounce
4 tablespoons = ¼ cup
5 tablespoons + 1 teaspoon
   = ⅓ cup
8 tablespoons = ½ cup
12 tablespoons = ¾ cup
16 tablespoons = 1 cup
1 cup = 8 ounces per ½ pint
4 cups = 1 quart
4 quarts = 1 gallon
6½ to 8-ounce can = 1 cup

10½ to 12-ounce can = 1¼ cups
14 to 16-ounce can (No. 300) = 1¾ cups
16 to 17-ounce can (No. 303) = 2 cups
1-pound 4-ounce can or 1-pint 2-ounce
   can (No. 2) = 2½ cups
1-pound 13-ounce can (No. 2½) =
3½ cups
3-pound 3-ounce can or 46-ounce can =
   5¾ cups
6½-pound or 7-pound 5-ounce can
   (No. 10) = 12 to 13 cups

Metric Equivalents

Liquid	**Dry**
1 teaspoon = 5 milliliters	1 quart = 1 liter
1 tablespoon = 15 milliliters	1 ounce = 30 grams
1 fluid ounce = 30 milliliters	1 pound = 450 grams
1 cup = 250 milliliters	2.2 pounds = 1 kilogram
1 pint = 500 milliliters	

NOTE: The metric measures are approximate benchmarks for purposes of home food preparation.

INDEX

This is a perfect
gift for Christmas, birthdays
or any occasion

★★★

You may order as many of our **Just Kid-ding Around** cookbooks as you wish for the price of $5.00 each plus $2.00 postage and handling per book ordered. Mail to:

Tennessee Chapter No. 21
Telephone Pioneers of America
Rm. 240 Green Hills Ofc. Bldg.
Nashville, Tennessee 37215

Save postage and handling charges by picking up your books at the Chapter Pioneer Office, Room 240 Green Hills Ofc. Bldg., Nashville, TN, Tel. No. 615-665-6792.

★★★

No. books ordered ______________
Amt. enclosed________________

Make check payable to: Telephone Pioneers

Please Print Clearly:

NAME____

ADDRESS ____

WORK ADDRESS ____

FLOOR OR ROOM NO. ____

CITY____

Telephone
Pioneers
of America
TELEPHONE PIONEERS OF AMERICA
ANSWERING THE CALL OF THOSE IN NEED